DATE DUE

JE 21 '95			
MR 14 '95			
MR 23 '95			
AP 5 '95			
AP 12 '95			
MY 24 '95			
JE 21 '95			
JE 28 '95			
JE 10 '96			
NO 25 '97			

SINGLE TREE

Also by Gary D. Svee

Sanctuary
Incident at Pishkin Creek
Spirit Wolf

SINGLE TREE

Gary D. Svee

Walker and Company
New York

All the characters and events portrayed in this work are fictitious.

First published in the United States of America in 1994 by Walker Publishing
Company, Inc.

Published simultaneously in Canada by Thomas Allen & Son Canada, Limited,
Markham, Ontario

Library of Congress Cataloging-in-Publication Data
Svee, Gary D., 1943–
Single tree / Gary D. Svee.
p. cm.
ISBN 0-8027-4142-8
1. Ranch life—Montana—Fiction. I. Title.
PS3569.V37S54 1994
813'.54—dc20 94-7536
CIP

Printed in the United States of America

2 4 6 8 10 9 7 5 3 1

Smiles, criticism, comfort, love:
This one's for you, Diane.

Author's Note

We must either gather up what stock we have left and leave the country or gather up these desperadoes and put them where they will kill and steal no more; there is no alternative, and we choose the latter. It is now simply a state of war.

—James Fergus, nineteenth-century cattleman

The vigilante movement of 1884 was aimed at cleaning out a nest of rustlers preying on herds of cattle and horses in Montana and Dakota. The story is obscure. The cattlemen were sworn to secrecy—to speak was to put a noose around their own necks, and good hemp rope choked off any comments from the rustlers. But it is estimated that the vigilantes killed more than sixty men that summer.

This novel is completely fictional, based loosely on later accounts of that story. The characters say the words that might have been spoken if the nooses had not silenced them.

SINGLE TREE

PROLOGUE

A SEED-BEARING BALL of fluff danced on the eddies and ripples of the northerly wind, bound for the eternal waters of the Missouri. Bright green leaves rustled in a century-old stand of cottonwoods, whispering the litany of the annual spring ritual.

Accept this seed, oh ageless river, giver of life.
Feed it with the silt of your spring waters, with the blood of
    the buffalo drowned in their crossing.
Grow then another stand of cottonwood trees to taste the
    breezes, to feel the nibble of the deer and the rub of the
    buffalo.
Do this and massive trees will shade your banks and keep
    you strong as you travel to the sea.

Below, the river bottom was white with millions of seeds, but only one caught a thermal rising off the black shale banks lining the river. Only one rode the northerly breeze beyond the river, over the prairie where no cottonwoods grew.

It floated above a patch of ground recently moistened by a thunderstorm. The seed settled here, tentative as a butterfly approaching a rose, and took root.

The sapling grew through the wet spring, its roots tracing moisture to an underground spring. Blessed by the gods, or chance, the cottonwood grew over the years, a patch of green on a prairie of yellow bunchgrass and silver sage and dark juniper. Unhampered by the shadows of taller trees, it spread wide its branches to embrace the sun.

The tree became a haven to the creatures of the high

1

plains. In summer, weary animals gratefully shared the tree's shade. In spring, buffalo, elk, and grizzly rubbed their hides against the cottonwood's rough gray bark, leaving sprigs of winter hair—as the plains tribes left willow wands and eagle feathers to commemorate their holy places.

The native people of the plains also came to stand in the tree's dark shadows to spy on rivers of passing buffalo, to seek their own kind—sailors traversing the sea of grass. Sometimes they left signs of their passing, a rock cairn or a hand painted red on a nearby boulder.

The cottonwood drew life to it with its promise of summer shade and water. And that is how it came to catch Sarah Wilders's eye one day in 1884.

CHAPTER 1

SAMUEL WILDERS'S TEETH grated together with each bump and jolt of the wagon. The road was little more than a trail, and previous wagons had worn all the soft out of it. Only the stones remained.

He could feel each of them through the steel-rimmed wagon wheels, through the long, unforgiving oaken spokes of the wheel, through the rock-hard seat that was wearing a hole in his soul.

He looked across the seat at his wife, Sarah. She swayed with each lurch of the wagon, her lap cushioning little Rosie from the wagon's abuse.

Seeing Sarah filled him with wonder. Even on the seat of this damnable wagon, even holding a squirming little girl, that woman seemed to be presiding over some wondrous cotillion. Whatever possessed her to marry a man like him, a man who would subject her to the indignities of the long trail from Nebraska to Montana?

Wilders pulled his eyes from his wife, and his mind from the guilt that had nagged at him for weeks. He turned his attention to the prairie. It was all here, just as Zeb Saunders had promised.

Saunders was a middle-aged cowboy—edging toward thirty—wandering south to pick up another herd when he rode into Friend, Nebraska. The vagaries of spring and chance drew the cowboy to the chair that sat empty most days in front of the Friendly Mercantile.

Chance and the need for seed brought Samuel Wilders to the store the same day. Wilders was a cowboy—a farmer's bib overalls and lace-up shoes couldn't hide that—and each man sensed a kindred spirit in the other.

The talk ranged up the long trail from Texas to Montana, Saunders talking about the rivers he crossed and the bad water and good whisky. But when he talked of Montana, he whispered almost reverently.

Montana was a place where the prairie bumped into the top of the world, Saunders said. Grass tall enough to scratch the belly of a horse, and the sky stretched from forever to forever. Didn't need land to raise cattle, just water. Find some unclaimed water and you had a ranch.

Saunders's words took root in Wilders's mind. Grass high as the belly of a horse, sky wide as forever . . . and Wilders would be doing what he did best, caring for cattle.

Wilders had spent most of his life on horseback. He would have been there still, if he hadn't found himself in Friend, Nebraska, years ago, fighting the granddaddy of all hangovers.

He awoke in the dark coolness of an alley with a splitting headache and empty pockets. He was ready to roar his anger, his frustration at humanity, when he saw the sun flash against golden hair: A princess was surveying her kingdom from the seat of a grain wagon. The sight of her pierced his heart as the morning sun had pierced his brain.

That was the day Samuel Wilders became a farmer. He stayed around Friendly and began to carve his living from the prairie with a single-bottom plow, his horizons shrinking to a plot of upside-down earth, to green plants peeking into the sun. And each day he appeared on the Johnson porch, tanned almost as dark as his boots, slim as the posts that held up the porch roof. He came carrying sprays of prairie flowers on his arm, carrying his heart on his sleeve.

And then she said yes, and her father smiled. The following year Jimmy Wilders squawked into the world. Samuel Wilders fell in love for the second time . . . and the third when little Rosie was born.

Wilders and his family attended a tiny steepled church each Sunday. During planting season, he prayed for a good crop, along with the rest of the congregation.

Nurture this seed, O Lord.

Quench its thirst with warm, gentle spring rains.

Bless it with the warmth of the sun so that it may grow green and strong and be a blessing to your creation.

Spare these fields, O Lord. Afflict them not with pestilence. Protect them from the hooves of passing cattle. Shelter them from searing winds and the hot hunger of prairie fire.

Do this, O Lord, and you will bless us with your giving and we will give in return to the needy who knock at our doors, in the tithing for the church.

Do this, O Lord, and we will sing your praise.

Wilders did his best to be a farmer. If that was what it took to win and keep Sarah Johnson Wilders, then that, by God, was what he would do.

Wilders worked at it, from before light to after dark. He worked himself thin as a rail and twice as hard, but Samuel Wilders was a cowboy. He would never be anything else.

His eyes were alight when he came home that day from the Mercantile and Zeb Saunders's stories. He told Sarah about Montana, tried to paint in her eyes the pictures he had seen in Saunders's words. She watched him then and watched him later, as he paced the kitchen that winter, as he stared from the kitchen window of the family's clapboard-sided farmhouse.

And then Sarah said yes, and Samuel glowed as he had when she had said yes to his proposal of marriage.

The excitement of their adventure grew until the two

felt almost giddy with their good fortune. When spring arrived, the Wilderses traded their farm for some breeding stock, a solid wagon, and hope. . . . They *clicked* the team north and west.

Sarah perched on the wagon seat and Samuel ranged free and easy on his saddle horse. They moved slowly, setting their pace to fit the herd's comfort. The weeks on the trail whittled them down, time and quicksand crossings and the constant breakdowns of the wagon. Their money disappeared first, and then their cattle, and then the saddle horses.

They were racing for their lives in a slow-moving wagon. They had to find an unclaimed creek and build a home. They would start slow, work brandings and roundups for a calf or two. They would make it: They had to.

They had just crossed the Missouri River in Montana and climbed the shale banks to the high plains. They were two days along that jolting, rocky road, just beginning to allow optimism to swell in their breasts when Jolly, one of the two horses pulling the Wilderses' wagon, dropped to his knee in a badger hole. The snap of the horse's leg cracked like the family's hopes, cracked like the rifle shot that stopped the animal's thrashing. Jack, the remaining draft horse, was too weak to pull the wagon very far alone.

It was then that Sarah Wilder saw the tree, a point of green against the blue horizon. Trees meant water. Water meant a place to bathe, coffee to drink, clean clothing. Trees meant shade from this god-awful heat, something to look at besides sagebrush, something to give definition to their lives.

It seemed to Sarah Wilders, even then, that they had been swallowed in the immensity of the prairie, an insignificant speck in a vastness that transcended imagination. Only the tree seemed real to her.

Wilders rigged the wagon for one horse and they walked behind it, following its creaking, final trek to the tree.

They found a dugout nearby where some trapper had wintered long ago. All the family needed was water enough to last while Wilders backtracked to the nearest ranch to find a second horse.

Samuel Wilders untied the shovel from the side of the wagon.

"Has to be a spring here," he said, more to himself than to his son, grunting as the first spadeful of earth tore loose from the rich prairie grass.

A vast swale tipped toward the cottonwood like a giant washbasin. Had to be water in that basin, Wilders thought. The cottonwood was proof. Cottonwoods are shallow-rooted, better suited to river bottom than prairie. The tree must be rooted in cool water from an underground spring.

Wilders grunted as another clump of grass and earth popped free.

"Has to be a spring here," he repeated to himself, wondering if that thought was dictated by the lay of the land or by his family's desperate need for water.

The fate of the Wilderses turned now with the clumps of dirt and prairie grasses. Another clump of grass tore loose. Blue grama, needle-and-thread, buffalo grass, and western wheat grass.

Samuel Wilders stopped, wiping the sweat from his brow with his shirtsleeve. The last clump of grass tore free in a circle five feet in diameter. Wilders wiped his forehead again with his sleeve and paused, stretching his neck. The digging would be easier now that he had broken through the grass cover.

Little puffs of dust arose as his heel slammed into the dry soil. As he dug deeper, it seemed that the prairie was consuming him just a little at a time, as the journey from Nebraska had consumed the family's possessions.

But he found damp soil and then a trickle of water and then a pool. He felt better, joking with Jimmy that if he had dug much deeper he might have fallen into an underground river and been swept around the world to emerge in China.

"Wouldn't those Chinese be surprised," Wilders said, "to see a blue-eyed devil pop from the earth?"

The next morning, he shuffled around the camp, spending as much time trying to read the light in his wife's eyes as he did packing for his journey. And when he could no longer postpone his leaving, he held Sarah Johnson Wilders at arm's length, trying to find the words that would extract forgiveness for placing her in this jeopardy.

She smiled, and he pulled her to him, their two bodies melding into one. Rosie came first to the hugging and then Jimmy, each seeking a part of the love they sensed.

Samuel Wilders mounted the draft horse and left the camp with a grin on his face, carrying his shotgun and pistol. He hoped to trade the weapons for a horse past its prime but willing still to help Jack pull the Wilderses toward their new home.

And that is how Sarah and Jimmy and Rosie came to settle by this lone tree on the prairie. They were carried there by chance, as the tree had been—and shallow rooted as the cottonwood, they remained.

The rider sat motionless, ringed by men from the Trident ranch. They had been waiting for him in a coulee, revealing themselves only when they were too close to be avoided, too near to run.

Samuel Wilders almost smiled. The draft animal was a poor choice for a race. Jack was capable of little more than a trot, and that for only short distances. The big-footed, roman-nosed horse was tired from the long trek, tired from pulling a rough-riding wagon.

Wilders's eyes flicked around the half circle of men— cowboys all, from their broad-brimmed hats to their down-at-the-heel boots. Their clothing was rough and mended.

Their meager pay was spent on wild hoorahs and not high fashion.

A grim-faced man with an air of command nudged his skittish roan forward. "Silas Tolkien," he growled. "Trident ranch."

"Sam Wilders. Saw your brand on some stock a ways back."

"Then what the hell are you doing here?"

"Just passing through."

"Where you headed?"

"Snowy Mountains. Friend said I might find a place to stake out for a little ranch up there."

"You going to start your ranch with that horse?"

Wilders tensed. He had seen enough cowboy courts to realize that he stood accused in one. "What the hell do you mean by that?"

"Mr. . . . ?"

"Wilders."

"Mr. Wilders, we've been watching you for half an hour."

Wilders bristled. "Spit it out."

"That's a Trident horse you're riding. We don't much care for rustlers, Mr. Wilders."

The hair went up on the back of Wilders's neck. He took off his hat and rubbed his sleeve across his forehead. "I'm no damn rustler. This is my gelding."

"You might explain the Trident brand on the right shoulder."

"It's not a trident, it's a pitchfork, registered in Nebraska to me."

The day was edging toward noon and hot, one of those days when the sun rubs out the horizon with its glare. Samuel Wilders's horizon was shrinking, too, from the vastness of the Montana prairie to the eyes of a half circle of grim men. Their faces were painted dark by the shadows of wide-brimmed hats. One of his accusers, a dark-haired, dark-skinned cowboy, looked away. That frightened Wilders more than all the glares. He sensed that the young man knew exactly what these men intended to do, and the kid couldn't look their victim in the eye.

Wilders had never thought of himself as a victim. He'd spent a wild youth on the plains of Texas. Even now his arms bore the puckered scars of flesh torn in thorn thickets. He was as much a cowboy as any of the men facing him, and he knew the seriousness of Tolkien's charge.

"Boys, he's telling us that he rode that plow horse all the way from Nebraska," Tolkien said.

Nervous laughter pattered through the men.

"Rides a plow horse, and he's armed to the teeth. Just what is it that you plan to do, boy, that you need a shotgun and a pistol to get it done?"

"I want to trade the pistol and the shotgun for another horse."

"Little George, he wants to trade those guns. Suppose you take them and we'll see what they're worth."

Wilders blanched and said, "Like hell."

"Son, you want to try to use those?"

"No."

"Then give them to Little George."

A florid-faced rider reined his horse next to Wilders, reaching over to take the weapons. Little George examined the weapons for a moment. "Not even loaded."

Tolkien's face, weathered parchment, wrinkled into what Wilders supposed was a grin.

"Hell of a rustler, boys. He doesn't even load his guns."

There was more nervous laughter.

"Son, we'd best stop at my office to talk this out."

"Listen, I need to trade for a horse. I left my family behind on the prairie. You have a horse you'll give me for the shotgun and pistol, we'll call it square."

The old man's face tightened. "We'll give you just what you deserve for stealing a Trident horse. We don't take rustling lightly in Montana."

"I left my family behind. I have to get back."

"You should have thought about that before you stole this horse."

"He's my horse. For God's sake, give me a chance to prove that." Wilders searched their faces, looking for compassion.

"Mr. Tolkien," said one of the men in the ring. "It wouldn't be much to backtrack this man. It would be easy enough to find out if he's telling the truth."

Tolkien's eyes squinted nearly shut. "Hell, a champion tracker like you, Mr. Gilfeather, you could probably track him back to his mama's womb. We could tell her we're awfully sorry that her son became a rustler."

"Better than not knowing, Mr. Tolkien."

"Maybe *you* don't know, Mr. Gilfeather, but I sure as hell do. Tie him up, boys, and we'll take him to my office."

Samuel Wilders's hands were tied behind his back. He sat astride his gelding and was led to the old man's "office" on the banks of Crazy Woman Creek, nothing more than a cattle-tramped meadow with a few cottonwood trees.

A rope sailed over a low-hanging limb above Wilders's head. "You can't do this! You can't do this to me! I'm no damn rustler."

The words came dead and deadly: "Hang him. Hang the son of a bitch."

The noose, thirteen coils in its killer knot, was pulled tight around Wilders's neck. Until that moment, he had thought that he might escape, that the madness would end. But he knew now that he was dead. His thoughts turned to Sarah and Jimmy and Rosie. They would never know what happened to him. They would wait beside that strange cottonwood tree for a husband and father who would never return.

Tears spilled from his eyes as he pleaded, "Tell my wife that I love her. Tell my children that I love them, that I didn't mean to leave them alone. Please . . . you must find them for me."

The old man blinked, and it seemed for a moment that he might reconsider. But Jack took that moment to step away to nibble at some fresh green grass, leaving his master kicking away his life at the end of the rope.

Tolkien watched until the kicks stopped and Samuel Wilders's face turned black for want of air.

CHAPTER 2

RUNS TOWARD FIDGETED in his sleep, his face reflecting the horror painted on the inside of his mind. The dream was the same. Grim men, visages black and white as skulls, surrounding a pleading man.

The man was dressed in a plaid flannel shirt and coarse wool pants. His boots and broad-brimmed hat were twins to those worn by his accusers. But their faces wore death, and his wonder and incomprehension.

The words came like chants in a camp revival: "I'm no damn rustler" sung soft and low, and then the chorus, atonal, one-noted and stretched out. "Hang-him-hang-the-son-of-a-bitch."

And when the rope went over his head, the man realized that he was dead. Tears ran from his eyes, and the executioners looked away. Cattlemen hanged only hardened rustlers. Hard cases didn't cry: They growled threats and curses, damned their executioners to hell. But this man gutted himself before his accusers, mourning his own death and the loss of his family.

Hard cases made killing easy. This killing was difficult. They might have yielded, washed soft by the man's tears. But then the roman-nosed work horse stepped off to taste a clump of bunch grass, green still in the spring sun. Its master, hands tied at the wrists, slipped off the horse's back, too softly to break his neck. His face contorted as he tried to squeeze air through his crushed throat. Since then, Runs Toward's dreams turned nightmarish. He was choking, unable to suck air into his own lungs as he watched this man die.

13

Runs Toward wanted to jerk his roan around to run from his dream, but the air seemed to have congealed, thickened to the consistency of syrup. Runs Toward's arm moved only with great effort and very, very slowly. The horse leaned into the turn, and so slowly did she move that for a moment it seemed that she must fall. Clods of dirt spun lazily from her driving hooves, hanging in the air like the ashes of burnt paper blowing in a soft breeze.

The horse rolled into a gallop, she and her rider leaning into viscous air, pushing to free themselves of a world inhabited by skulls, running from the contorted face of the man hanging from the tree. But the run was slow, slow as fluff falling from a cottonwood tree.

Runs Toward tried to suck fresh air into his lungs. His face contorted with the effort. The hanging seemed to have crushed his throat, too, leaving his face blackened by suffocation. He was dying for want of air, for want of speed.

A thought tickled Runs Toward's brain. He should awaken now. This was where he always awoke, blankets in a tangle on the rough wood floor, breath coming in gasps, a sheen of sweat covering him like a silk sheet.

But the horse ran on, and Runs Toward realized that he could not escape. He was borne along by forces beyond his ken and control. He could only grip the horse with his knees, hoping the animal would not leave him to drown in his dream.

Then he saw the tree, standing alone on the prairie, miles from its nearest brother, spreading is limbs wide to catch the kiss of the sun. The tree was magic. Runs Toward knew that as certainly as he knew that he must go to it.

The horse ran in a slow-motion gallop. The tree stood now nearly a mile away, and as Runs Toward drew near, he saw some men gathered beneath it. Closer he came, and the tree grew black, like a silhouette on a starlit night. Beneath the tree were men, their visages ashen and hollow-eyed as skulls.

Runs Toward tried to pull his mare away from her terrifying course, from this maddening run, but on and on she flew. Not even as the horse neared the men did she stop. She ran toward her twin standing beneath the tree, eager to deliver her rider to his destiny.

Runs Toward stopped sawing at the reins when he saw the man beneath the tree. Suddenly he felt himself melding with the man—he felt the rub of rough hemp rope against his own throat. He was the center of attention now. It was he with a loop around his neck. It was he seeking compassion and justice from these stranglers.

Runs Toward heard a chorus of "Hang him. Hang him higher than Haman. Higher than Haman."

Runs Toward wanted to scream, but the rope . . .

"Runs Toward . . . Runs Toward." The words were accompanied by a gentle shaking. The young man stirred and his eyes popped opened, peering through the darkness of the bunkhouse.

"Let's have a smoke."

The terror on Runs Toward's face eased as he recognized his friend Eli Gilfeather. He nodded, shivering a little as he felt the cold air. He awakened as he had for more than a month, covered with sweat, blankets strewn on the floor.

Runs Toward slipped into his trousers. He paused to run a towel over his upper body, shivering again in the chill before slipping his shirt over his head. His hand found his tobacco sack and papers to serve a habit he had acquired from Gilfeather.

As he stepped outside, he saw the red glow of a cigarette, and Gilfeather's silhouette standing against the corral. Eli would be leaning against the top pole, right foot resting atop the bottom pole. Eli Gilfeather was a creature of habit, and that was how he usually stood.

Runs Toward's hands were shaking as he tried to roll his cigarette. Tobacco spilled invisible toward the ground. "Chilly," he said.

"Yeah, chilly."

Runs Toward could see Gilfeather's hat, outlined by stars, swing toward him. He knew Gilfeather's brown eyes would be wide open, appraising.

"Same dream?" Gilfeather asked.

"Yeah . . ." Runs Toward hesitated. "No. Not exactly."

Gilfeather fell silent. After a while Runs Toward said solemnly. "They're going to hang me. I saw it in the dream. They're going to hang me like they hanged him."

"You dreamed that?"

"I could feel the rope. I've never let anyone put a rope around my neck, but I know exactly what it feels like. I felt it in the dream. They're going to hang me, Eli. They're going to hang me higher than Haman."

The words sounded flat and dead, and Gilfeather cleared his throat before replying. "You've done nothing."

"Doesn't matter. That man didn't do anything wrong, either, and they hanged him."

"It's different with you."

"No different." Runs Toward hesitated again. "I think they're going to hang you, too."

Gilfeather's cigarette dropped in the darkness like a falling star. Runs Toward could hear Gilfeather's heel crushing the ember to death, and then the rustle as he rolled another cigarette. The rich smell of tobacco teased Runs Toward's nose for a moment, and he remembered that he hadn't finished rolling his own.

"Did you dream that too?" Gilfeather asked.

"That you'd be hanged?" Runs Toward could see Gilfeather nod against the backdrop of stars. "No, but I think they will hang you."

"Have you heard anything?" Gilfeather's voice had a strange edge to it.

"No."

"Then it's just like your dream. It doesn't mean anything."

"Come with me. We'll go north to my people."

"You think they will remember you after all these years?"

"No, but they will remember my father and my mother, and they will remember the black robe and the time he led us Christians to the Musselshell River."

Runs Toward would never forget that time.

The air was frozen, tiny ice crystals hanging like fog over the Musselshell River's bottom. The air stung the nose with each breath; it hid the tiny Cree village from the world. The band had come to the valley four days ago like wraiths, skeletal people on starving horses, following a white man who was cloaked black as a raven.

They had ridden into Montana on the north wind and sometimes, when the wind blew the snow around, the man in black would disappear from their view. With him would disappear the people's hope that they would find nourishment. But always the man reappeared and always the people followed. They were trekking south away from their homes in Canada, from the cold arms of the mother queen.

The Missouri was frozen hard as stone as they crossed; the clatter of hooves was deadened by the cold. The cold deadened everything in Montana: warmth and sight and life.

The Cree band was special: They were Christians. They had seen a spirit smoldering, flickering and blazing in the Father's wild, spellbinding eyes. Father Reardon had been touched by the spirit and they were touched by him.

The time had come, he said, to test their newfound faith. The Cree Christians were to leave behind all but the essentials of shelter and a modicum of food and follow him. Follow they did, south, across the Montana border through a killing cold. Always ahead of them strode that black-cloaked figure.

When they reached the Musselshell, the priest pronounced their faith fit, even as their bodies shriveled with cold and hunger. Seeing the suffering in their eyes, he declared, too, that the white man's cattle were God's gift for Cree bellies.

They killed four steers, a cow, and a calf. They butchered also the first of their horses to die as they prepared to celebrate their sacrifice.

Sacrifice came naturally to the Cree. Once, ages ago, a bitter cold ruled the world, fiercer even than cutting winds they now suffered. Send the sun, the Cree prayed, and every year in the month of the poplars they would make sacrifices to their god.

But what was a suitable sacrifice to the Cree god? Since he was the creator of all things, he was also the owner of all things—except pain. Only pain belonged to his people. So they sacrificed their pain, sticking skewers beneath cut flaps of their skin. The skewers were tied then to the "enemy," a pole or buffalo skulls representing evil, and they tugged until their flesh tore loose.

The people understood well the need to sacrifice pain to their god, but never had they experienced pain like this on their journey of faith. The Christian God must be powerful indeed. So they celebrated their sacrifice and the Christian God's great power in a feast. But when the feast was finished and the cattle consumed, the cold remained.

Horses, unable to reach grass through the earth's frozen mantle of snow, stripped willows and cottonwood of their bark. But the bark merely prolonged the inevitable. As the horses died, they were eaten—poor, stringy meat for a dying people.

And when the people had given all they could, the Christian God demanded still more.

A band of riders appeared one cloudy day. The newcomers were led by a stern-faced man with a beard that reached to the bottom of his ribs. Runs Toward, so named because he feared nothing, thought the man was the Christian God come to rescue his people.

But the man was a rancher, and he came to kill. He spoke only one word, "Who?" and the muzzle of his rifle swung to frozen cattle hides hanging over ropes in the camp. Talking Bird, leader of the band, said, "The Father told us we could kill cattle if we were starving."

"Bring him here."

Talking Bird scurried off, returning a moment later with Father Reardon. Reardon raised his hands to bless the visitor and was cut short.

"If you take one more head of cattle, I will hang you higher than Haman."

The words were harsh, deadly, and Father Reardon's face blanched white as snow. No more words were said that day. The bearded man and his riders picked the six strongest horses from the band's tiny herd, one for each butchered beef, and drove them away.

Caught on the prairie with no provisions and with the remaining horses too weak to hunt, the band died little by little. They butchered the horses while they lasted, and later made "soup" of boiled rawhide.

At the end Father Reardon huddled with the band, promising them eternal life in a land of plenty. They listened in awe of the Christian God: How powerful he must be to exact such terrible suffering from his people.

The little village died slowly, as though it were going to sleep, and when death closed the Crees' eyes, the wolves came. Runs Toward heard them growling, fighting over the softest parts of the people in Buffalo Rubs Him's lodge. They circled the village, claiming the bodies in the lodges around the edge of the camp, working their way toward the tepee where the ten-year-old boy waited.

Runs Toward didn't see his mother die. Her spirit fled the frigid Montana prairie during the night, shutting out forever the sounds of wolves cracking the bones of her friends.

Runs Toward's father awakened the next morning to find Rose Hip lying dead beside him. Bull Runs, weak and feverish, turned his wide, jaundiced eyes to look at his son. He smiled at Runs Toward and then his head fell back in death.

The wolves whined nearby. Runs Toward could hear the frantic pad of soft feet as the hungry predators came closer to him.

On the third day, a wolf poked his head through the tepee flap. The male, gray and black with yellow eyes, seemed not the vicious predator so much as a harvester checking his crop. The wolf's eyes and nose searched the darkness, until they caught the glint of Runs Toward's eyes. The two animals stared into each other's souls.

Runs Toward knew that he was staring at his own death, and with that knowledge came a calmness, a great relief from the terror that had been his only companion since his parents died. He began to sing, his voice weak and throat dry. He sang about his life and his mother and father. He sang about his acceptance of the Christian God. He asked to meet his parents in the land where the buffalo still ran.

The wolf turned away to rejoin the rest of the pack.

When the tepee flap was opened again later that morning, Runs Toward tried again to sing his death song, but he didn't have the strength and he could not remember the words. He hoped it was the wolf with the golden eyes come to claim him, death being more easily met in the presence of a friend.

But Eli Gilfeather opened the lodge flap. Ice tugged at his long, black beard and his breath trickled like smoke from his nose. Fire and ice.

Gilfeather brought life to Runs Toward. The cowboy had answered a call he didn't understand that day. For some reason he could not explain, he had left his line cabin that morning to venture into the bitter cold. He was drawn to that camp on the Musselshell, that camp marked for death by wolf tracks and the absence of smoke.

The cowboy's eyes roved past the corpses in the tepee and stopped on Runs Toward. The boy, black eyes glittering from a pile of buffalo robes, seemed one faltering breath from the other side.

Eli found wood and built a fire in the lodge, brewing a weak broth of the beef jerky he carried in his saddlebags. The boy's head wobbled with weakness, so Eli held the boy up so he could drink the broth. As the boy slept, Eli built a scaffold in the cottonwood trees along the Musselshell. He wrapped Runs Toward's family in buffalo robes and placed them on the scaffold, saying a few words from what he remembered of the Good Book. He might not have done that had he not seen a black cloak and clerical collar near wolf-ravaged bones.

As Runs Toward grew stronger, Eli learned that the boy spoke English. They talked, and Runs Toward agreed to go to Eli's line cabin. That was the day Eli found his son. That was the day Runs Toward became a white man.

Gilfeather sighed, his breath whistling between his teeth. "Old man Tolkien has been acting funny, lately," he said to Runs Toward in the night air. "Every time I look up he's staring at me. He keeps me close to the ranch. I don't know what he's thinking, but he gives me the willies.

"And Jimmy Pearson from the DHS ranch stopped by. Cattlemen at the association meeting this spring were saying they're losing as many as one out of every ten head to rustlers. Rumor is that the cattlemen intend to put together a band of vigilantes to tour eastern Montana and western North Dakota.

"You know what that means, Runs Toward?"

"No."

"It's a hanging party. They'll string up everyone suspected of being a rustler. They'll string up everyone they find on the open range, just like that one fellow we found—what was it, a month ago?"

"Five weeks and three days," Runs Toward whispered.

Gilfeather faced him and took another drag on his cigarette. The embers lit his face in dark, ominous shadows, his forehead wrinkled in concern. "Didn't tell you about this because I wanted to have everything ready before we made the jump.

"I was riding way out one day, trailing a bunch of strays that someone was taking north. I came across a little creek that has rims to the north; it would protect us from those hellacious winter winds and give us a front door open to chinooks and spring sun. Good grass. Enough trees for shelter, but not so heavy that you'd wear a horse out hazing the cattle from it. Runs about three miles and disappears into the prairie.

"That's where we'll stake out our ranch, Runs Toward. Didn't want to tell you about it until I had everything in place, and you know as well as I do that we can't file on it until we get some money."

An owl screeched in the night, and both men stopped to listen. Gilfeather broke the silence.

"Hell, Runs Toward, we'll never save enough wages to start our own place. Maybe if we worked for Granville Stuart. He lets his cowboys run their own stock on his place. . . . But we don't work for Granville Stuart.

"So . . . I . . . I've . . . I've been talking to Stringer Jack's bunch."

Runs Toward jerked around to face Gilfeather. "No!"

"Shhh! Quiet, boy, or they'll hang me right now." Gilfeather's voice took on a conciliatory tone. "Hell, it ain't like I'm the only one. They've got a man or two on every ranch in the territory. And I never drive a single steer off Trident land. All I do is tell someone every couple of weeks where the cattle are and the men aren't. That's all. Stringer gives me a double eagle every time."

Gilfeather's voice was touched with excitement now. "Runs Toward, I got close to three hundred dollars. With the two hundred you and me saved, that's damn near enough. A couple more months and we could slip off and start our own place.

"But, I think Tolkien is on to me. At least, he's suspicious."

Runs Toward straightened and then leaned toward Gilfeather. "Come with me to my people in Canada. We'll be safe there. We can leave now."

"If I run now, Old Man Tolkien will send the stranglers after me. They'll hang me sure as hell."

"And me?"

"If they found you with me . . . Runs Toward, you better go. Get your pay, and I'll give you half of our savings. If I get loose of this, I'll come north to find you. You can leave word at Fort Mcleod."

CHAPTER 3

ELI GILFEATHER HESITATED in front of the bunkhouse. He had spent a restless night, speeches running through his mind since Runs Toward announced that he was leaving. But speeches were only words and the young Cree was part of his life. How could he tell Runs Toward that?

Gilfeather squinted up at the sun and sighed. The day was running away from him. He took a deep breath and stomped through the door of the bunkhouse, waiting a moment for his eyes to adjust to the dim light.

Runs Toward knelt beside his bunk, rolling his bedroll as tightly as he could across the worn mattress. Gilfeather took a seat on an adjoining bunk, watching the young man work.

"Better not sit there," Runs Toward said. "Jake will have a fit if he sees you on his cot."

"They sent Jake up on Crazy Woman Creek."

"What about you?"

"Charley gave me a little time . . . to say good-bye."

"Charley's all right."

"Yeah."

Eli reached across the cot and snatched a pair of socks Runs Toward was about to put into his pack.

"I didn't teach you a damn thing, did I."

"What do you mean?"

"Look at the holes in these socks. You have to walk anywhere, your boots will wear a hole right through your feet."

"Don't intend to walk anywhere."

"We do a hell of a lot of things we don't intend to do, kid."

"Yeah, I know. Like hang people."

"You didn't have anything to do with that."

"I didn't do anything to stop it. At least you tried."

"Hell, it wouldn't have made any difference. Old Man Tolkien had his mind set on a hanging. Wasn't anything we could do."

"I don't know that. I just know that I didn't do anything. At least you suggested we might backtrack him." Runs Toward looked up at Eli. "Do you think he was a rustler?"

Gilfeather fidgeted for a moment on the cot. "What the hell?" He reached beneath the straw-filled mattress and pulled out a pint of whisky. "No wonder Jake's so touchy about anyone sitting on his cot."

Eli popped the cork and sniffed. "Whoo-ee, that is four-bit whisky. Four bits a gallon if you can find a taker. You want a swig?"

Runs Toward shook his head.

"No, not me, either."

"Do you think he was a rustler, Eli?"

Eli rubbed his hand across the stubble on his cheek, "No. Poor son of a bitch."

"Yeah."

"What did Old Man Tolkien say when you told him you were leaving?"

"He grinned."

"Grinned?"

"Like he knew something I didn't."

"Hope the hell he doesn't know about . . ."

"Yeah. Why don't you come with me, Eli?"

"I don't think he'd let both of us go. He's suspicious, and if we both lit out, he'd figure that was proof."

"Proof enough for a hanging, anyway."

"Yeah."

Runs Toward stood, slinging his gear over his shoulder.

"Hell, I came to give you a hand. All the years we've been together and you can carry everything you've got over one shoulder."

Runs Toward reached out to take Eli's shoulders in his hands. He stared into his white father's eyes. "You gave me life, Eli. That's worth something, isn't it?"

Eli looked away to stare out one of the bunkhouse's dusty windows. "There was some reason you survived that time on the Musselshell. It wasn't just luck that led me to you."

"Eli . . ."

"Yeah."

"I don't think we'll ever see each other again."

"Oh, hell, boy, don't say that. We'll meet up in Canada like we planned. We'll start that ranch we talked about."

"I think they're going to hang me, Eli. I don't know why, but I think they will."

Eli was shaking his head, denying the words, denying the certainty in Runs Toward's voice. "Nothing for you to worry about, boy. You've got the bills of sale for those two horses, don't you?"

Runs Toward nodded. He lowered his gaze. When he looked up at Gilfeather his eyes were glistening. "Eli, I am leaving my father."

Runs Toward's face was lost in Eli's own tears. He turned away so Runs Toward wouldn't see them. When he spoke, his voice was distorted by the constriction in his throat. "And I am losing my only son." He turned on his heel, then, and disappeared out the door of the bunkhouse.

The sandstone butte was a tiny island of rock emerging from a sea of grass. It tugged at Runs Toward's eye and his imagination, and finally he pointed the mare's nose toward it.

The rock had been whittled over the centuries by Montana's harsh winters and howling winds. Flat on top and fractured on the sides, the butte poked twelve feet higher than the scattering of old boulders and prairie grasses at its feet.

Runs Toward reined his mare into the butte's shade and leaned against the side of the rock, his fingers seeking cracks in the weathered surface to steady himself. He shook his feet loose from the stirrups and climbed onto his saddle, crouching at first. Then he stood, his fingers scrabbling up the stone to steady himself. Standing erect on the back of his horse, he could reach the top of the rock, so he scrambled up.

Runs Toward stood, the sun scratchy on his face, the breeze gentle as a kiss. His nose was filled with the scent of the sacred sage, and he peered out at the thin blue line where earth meets the heavens.

When his mind was free of everything but the beauty of the prairie, he prayed to be free of the dream that haunted him, the vision of the man as the rope choked the life from him. He prayed that on this journey he would find peace.

Jimmy Wilders sat in the shade of the lone cottonwood, his back propped against the rough gray bark. Outside that cone of coolness, he could feel the heat, a palpable creature pervading the sun-drenched prairie.

Jimmy had won his race with the sun that morning, arising before it cracked the eastern horizon. He dressed in darkness, slipping his sling and five precious, egg-shaped stones into the one pocket sturdy enough still to carry them.

The boy had already walked more than two miles from the dugout when the sun peeped over the horizon. He carried the sling dangling from his right hand, one leather thong looped around his middle finger and the other clasped between his thumb and forefinger. His ammunition, one of the egg-shaped rocks, pulled sweat from the palm of his left hand.

He walked as quietly as he could through prairie grass, the crisp scent of sage strong in his nose.

A herd of antelope skipped yellow and white across his vision. He saw not the beauty of their passing but raw meat for the fire.

If he had any ammunition for his rifle, he would have dropped to the ground behind that juniper and teased the curious animals into range with the flash of his shirt. But he had no ammunition. He had used it all in the first two weeks of their isolation, when he had still believed that his father would return. His eyes teared and his vision blurred at the thought of his father. He shook his head to clear it.

The responsibility of providing meat for his mother and five-year-old sister rested heavily on his twelve-year-old shoulders. He had no time to think about his father.

He tried to ignore the antelope as they trickled out of sight, watching instead for the heads and necks of prairie chickens, taking a fatal peek over the grass at this strange, two-legged creature. Perhaps a sage hen, tough as a juniper post and nearly as smart, would stalk through a stand of sage, hesitating too long to lumber into the air.

Sage hen meat was stringy and hard to chew, but covered with the little prairie onions Rosie dug when he was gone and baked slow—everything baked slow on fires built of buffalo chips—the bird was edible.

Jimmy wondered if this would be the day when he found no birds or rabbits or snakes. He had dreamed of eating giant grasshoppers, carving them as he might carve a turkey and serving them to his horrified mother and little sister. Even now, as they clicked away from his every step, he imagined them frying in a pan. He was so hungry . . . and the insects were so plentiful.

He walked slowly, stopping often to watch for the flick of a jackrabbit's ear before it ran for its life. Need and constant practice with the sling had given Jimmy the edge he needed. Just a moment of hesitation and a hare was meat in the pot.

But no jackrabbits flicked their ears. No sage hens craned their necks to see the intruder. No rattlesnakes buzzed their greetings of death.

So Jimmy returned, empty-handed and empty-bellied. He would tell his sister Rosie that he had spotted game and that he would be going back in the evening to collect meat. Perhaps she would not cry, then.

Back at the dugout, Jimmy stopped at the spring. He remembered helping his father, seeing the sheen of sweat on the elder Wilders's face as he dug for life-giving water on the Montana prairie so many weeks ago.

Rosie was playing alone in the spring, making mud pies. The little girl with curly red hair and freckles more pronounced in the sun had grown skinny in these past six weeks. Her hair poked in spears from her head; her skin and dress were mottled with mud and sweat and stains of unknown origin. She played slowly, as though movement required great effort.

If their mother could see her now: Jimmy shook his head. Sarah Wilders spent most of her time in the dugout.

Rosie reached for the rusting pan she used to "bake" her mud pies, and something fell from her pocket, glinting in the sun.

Jimmy stiffened. He scrambled to his feet and walked toward Rosie, his eyes pinned on the cylindrical object lying in the dust. Rosie looked up quizzically as he approached. "Want some apple pie?" she asked holding out her pan.

Jimmy shuddered. Mud ringed Rosie's mouth, and the boy realized that his sister actually had been eating her mud pies.

Rosie noticed then that Jimmy's eyes dropped to the ground by her feet. Her hand raced his for the .44-40 cartridge. Jimmy's won, and Rosie began to cry.

"That's mine," she said, sobbing. "That's my pretty."

Jimmy's voice was tight. "Do you have any more pretties, Rosie?"

Rosie shook her head, rendered mute at the thought of losing her only treasure.

"Wouldn't you trade your pretty for a dinner where you could have all you wanted to eat?"

Rosie thought for a moment and then nodded.

"I'll take your pretty, then, and get us something to eat. Okay?"

Rosie stared at her brother for what seemed to be forever and then nodded. Jimmy went toward the wagon to get his rifle.

Jimmy followed his morning's track away from the wagon, seeing evidence of his passing in bent grass and an occasional heel print in a patch of bare ground. He carried a rope coiled around one shoulder and a half-full canteen over the other.

He could feel the heat of the sun on his face. Settling as it was on the western horizon, it seemed close enough to touch, close enough to feel its warmth as he had felt the warmth of his mother's cookstove in Nebraska.

Nebraska and the family's farm seemed like a dream, a place with clothing that smelled fresh from the sun, where beds were soft and warm, where each night the family met at a table covered with food.

Jimmy bit his lip, using the pain to draw his mind away from his hunger. Jimmy was tired, tired from his long walk in the morning, tired of listening to his belly cry for food.

The boy's feet seemed to drag across the prairie, grass clutching at them, resisting his passing. His gait obstructed by the fierce pressure of responsibility, the ache of hunger.

Movement flashed across the corner of Jimmy Wilders' eye. Something gray exploded from a clump of sagebrush. Jimmy turned, sweeping the rifle to his shoulder, nestling the stock against his cheek. He glimpsed a blur of movement, and his eyes framed the thin blade on the muzzle in the buckhorn rear sight.

The rifle was heavy, not designed for twelve-year-old arms and shoulders, but it felt light today.

When the jackrabbit stopped, Jimmy framed the front sight in the buckhorn and set the hare's eye on the top of the blade, like an apple on a fence post. At this distance, he could shoot the jackrabbit in the eye. He knew he could. He knew he would eat tonight.

Jimmy's thumb eased the hammer back toward full cock, and then his eyes closed and he slid the hammer back to half cock and safety. Only one bullet lay between the Wilderses and starvation. Jimmy didn't dare use it on a jackrabbit. He had to seek bigger game—a deer or an antelope.

But he could use his sling! He carried the sling and rocks with him everywhere. Jimmy's hand slid into his pocket and his eyes opened in slits. But the hare was gone, slipped beyond his view.

The boy's body sagged. He threw his head back and tears ran down his face. He wanted desperately to fall on the prairie grass, to give up, but if he failed to find food the rest of the family would disappear from the face of the earth as his father had.

Jimmy dried his face and settled the butt of his rifle on the prairie. He rested the loop of his sling over his middle finger and clasped the other thong between his thumb and index finger. One of his egg-shaped rocks was in the palm of his right hand. Then he hoisted his rifle into the crook of his left arm, steadying its weight against his chest with his right hand. He was ready now for deer or antelope or jackrabbits.

Jimmy drew a long breath and stretched the stiffening muscles of his neck. At that moment he caught the flicker of movement ahead. Jimmy dropped out of sight behind a juniper bush and waited.

The band of antelope stood at the crest of a small hill. They cautiously scanned the prairie.

Jimmy made a slight movement to catch their attention without frightening them.

The herd stood still. A doe and two fawns yielded to their curiosity. They took a few tentative steps toward this peculiar, beckoning creature. The herd followed, stopping periodically to nibble at the prairie grasses, fawns gamboling in the prairie sun.

Jimmy Wilders waited in the bush's shadow, afraid the antelope would hear the beating of his heart. If the antelope continued their tentative approach to the bush, if the wind didn't shift, if his thumping heart didn't burst, he would have only one shot—just one shot to bring death to an antelope, and life to him and his mother and his sister.

Jimmy waved his shirt again. The doe started and shook her head.

She's going to run, Jimmy thought. *She's going to run and I'll have to take a running shot. No—if she runs, I let her go.* The bullet was too precious to risk.

The herd took a few more steps toward the bush. The wind was holding, carrying Jimmy's scent away from them. What could that odd creature in the juniper bush be?

The antelope were about two hundred yards from the bush now. Jimmy might be able to hit them at that distance, but the .44-40 had a trajectory shaped like an Indian's bow. A shot that long relied more on luck than skill. Jimmy couldn't take that chance.

As the herd approached, one tentative step after another, the doe and the two fawns continued to lead the way. At a hundred yards, Jimmy raised his rifle. It felt as heavy as the crowbar Jimmy had used to help his father dig out the spring. But heavy as it was, the barrel wavered with the slightest gust of wind and the sights bobbed and weaved before Jimmy's desperate eyes.

The doe was just seventy-five yards away now. Jimmy could wait no longer. He pressed cheek against the rifle's oiled stock, braced his arms against his knees. He was focusing on the sights when he saw the fawns playfully butting heads at their mother's side. Soon they would be orphans—orphans like Rosie and him, with their father gone and their mother off inside herself where they couldn't reach her.

Suddenly tears filled Jimmy's eyes and Jimmy couldn't see. *Damn it!* he thought, blinking hard to clear his eyes. He saw the herd dancing, nervous. Something was wrong! They were going to run! If they ran . . .

Jimmy caught the flash of black, front-thrust horns, a buck! He tried to set the rifle's bobbing sights on the buck's shoulder before the animals ran. The rifle barked. Jimmy's shoulder rocked back, and his eyes were jerked with the muzzle's recoil to the clouds. When his eyes returned to earth, he saw the band of antelope running, streaming away.

He must have missed. *Damn you, Jimmy Wilders! You killed your mother and your sister and yourself! Damn you, Jimmy Wilders.*

The antelope were running in a string with the does and fawns to the front of stiff-legged bucks. One of the bucks stumbled and then fell on the prairie. His legs twitched—and then they were still.

Jimmy Wilders wept, tears sheeting his face, scrubbing off a layer of mud made of dust and sweat. His face was shining as he raised his eyes and thanked his God for the Wilderses' good fortune. Tonight Rosie would eat real meat.

CHAPTER 4

RUNS TOWARD WAS in his third day away from the Trident ranch, a day that shimmered in the heat of the June sun. The sun bleached the color from the land, leaving it without form or depth—except for a black spot on the horizon. Black is the Cree color for death, and Runs Toward tried to ignore it, but no one can ignore death.

His sorrel mare waded through the heat, her head drooping with the effort, but her steady gait carried him ever closer to the shadow, which slowly took shape for Runs Toward.

A cottonwood, but no cottonwood would grow on this treeless prairie. This was a land of prickly pear and juniper and yucca and grass, not cottonwoods.

As he drew nearer to the tree his eyes widened in recognition. This was the tree of his dreams. His sun-blanched eyes peered into the shadows beneath the tree, seeking the men with faces like skulls and a rope woven for death.

Jimmy Wilders stood vigilant on the prairie, half a mile from the dugout, his body tense, as he stared at the lone horseman. Hope surged through the boy and then died as he realized that the rider was too tall and lithe to be his father.

However, the horseman might be carrying word of his father. Maybe old Jack had thrown him, and he was laid up somewhere with a broken leg. Maybe Samuel Wilders had sent help.

Then Jimmy thought maybe not.

He thought about his little sister and mother at the dugout—helpless. That was when he started running for the dugout. He had the edge, the horseman was still a mile away, but the stranger had four legs to carry him and Jimmy had only two.

Runs Toward saw the tiny stick figure running ahead of him. Then, he saw a rough dugout and a wagon languishing in the sun beneath the tree. That was wrong.

His dream held no dugout and wagon, but this was the tree of his dreams. He felt certain of that.

The running figure disappeared into the shadow beneath the tree. No telling how many of them there were hiding in that shadow. But it couldn't be the stranglers. No horses waited on the prairie, so Runs Toward rode on, his eyes probing the darkness beneath the tree.

Children, a boy and a girl alone on the prairie. Runs Toward reined the sorrel to a stop.

Jimmy Wilders and Rosie stood like statues between the young man and the spring and the old wagon, almost hidden in a swale.

Jimmy was holding the rifle in the crook of his arm, and Runs Toward was well aware that the rifle's hammer was drawn to full cock.

The children must be alone, Runs Toward thought. Dirt, sweat, and dried mud coated the little girl. Her hair, some shade of red hidden beneath a layer of grime, was in a tangle poking from her head like quills from a frightened porcupine.

She was wearing a pink dress with a bow in the back and a lace fringe around the neck, so stained that little of the pink was visible.

The boy, burnt brown from the summer sun, was clad in tattered jeans and shirt. His black shoes, scuffed brown on the toes and heels, were tied on by knotted laces.

Runs Toward guessed the boy was between ten and twelve—not particularly tall, but wiry. His face showed concern, but no fear. Runs Toward knew the boy would swing the muzzle of the old Winchester on him without a moment of hesitation.

"I'd like to water my horses," Runs Toward said.

"Bucket by the spring. Don't let them into the spring. That's our drinking water."

Runs Toward nodded and swung down from the horse, slowly. He left the mare and gelding ground-reined and stepped toward the spring. The sorrel followed him.

Rosie piped up, "I'll hold your horse for you, mister."

Jimmy grabbed his little sister by the arm, almost losing control of his rifle with the effort. "You stay put, Rosie."

Rosie twisted free and ran toward the horse. As she neared, Runs Toward was more aware than ever that the little girl badly needed a bath. He handed the reins to her and stepped to the spring, picking up a new galvanized bucket lying in the prairie grass. He dipped the bucket in the water and carried it to his roan.

The mare emptied the bucket in long slurps, and Runs Toward carried water to the packhorse. When both horses had drunk their fill, he returned to the spring and stripped off his shirt. He scooped cool water on his face and neck shoulders and arms, washing sweat and dust and heat free of him. Only after his ablutions did he cup his hands together and sip some water.

When he finished, Runs Toward dipped his shirt in the bucket of water, wringing it almost dry before donning it. He stepped into the shade of the cottonwood tree, his eyes following the rough trunk upward. About twelve feet above, a thick limb reached out, almost parallel with the ground. The limb was scarred where some long-ago wind had nipped off a branch, leaving a nubbin pointing skyward.

This was the hanging tree. No doubt about that.

Just then the door to the dugout scraped open. A woman in her early thirties stepped out, blinking in the bright light. Her skin was bleached white by the darkness of the dugout. Eyes blue as the sky, but without the spark of life, overlooked a finely chiseled nose in a face surrounded by blond hair.

The woman's eyes slipped past her daughter and son. The sound of a man's voice had drawn her unwilling into the light to look for her husband.

Her eyes settled for a moment on Runs Toward.

"Oh, I see," she said. Her hands fluttered nervously to her hair. "I'm sorry, I didn't . . . My husband should be here by now, I can't understand . . ."

The woman ducked her head and fled into the dugout.

Runs Toward followed her. The dugout was a jerry-rigged combination of dirt and rock and lodge poles. It smelled of earth.

Runs Toward was about to step in when he felt the muzzle of the boy's rifle stab his back.

"Get away from there," Jimmy said. "You stay away from my mother."

Runs Toward turned slowly as Jimmy stepped back to keep the rifle safe from Runs Toward's reach.

"You've watered your horses. It's time for you to be moving on."

"Ease up, son. I wouldn't hurt anyone."

"I'm not your son."

"Who are you?" Runs Toward asked.

"None of your business."

Rosie, riding the energy of a bellyful of antelope, said, "His name's Jimmy."

"Hush, Rosie."

"Can't make me."

"Can too."

"Can't either."

Jimmy realized that in being pulled into a childish game, he had revealed his own childishness. His embarrassment showed through his deep tan. He tried to make his voice low and gruff, but it squeaked. "Git on out of here, mister."

"Runs Toward. My name is Runs Toward."

"I don't care what your name is. Just git!"

Rosie poked her finger at Jimmy. "He hasn't got any pretties, anyway."

"Pretties?" Runs Toward asked.

"Pretties to shoot in the gun. I had the last pretty, and he shot an antelope with it."

"She's lying," Jimmy said, sucking his lips between his teeth.

"That's a lie, Jimmy. You shouldn't lie." Rosie's mouth puckered.

"You need some help, Jimmy."

"No. You just git!" Jimmy reached into his pocket, retrieved his sling and slipped the open loop over his finger. He pulled a rock from his left pocket and slipped it into the leather pocket on the sling.

Jimmy was spinning the rock now, slowly, his eyes never leaving Runs Toward's face.

"Go now!" Jimmy growled. "Or you won't go at all."

Runs Toward's voice dropped almost to a whisper. "You don't really mean that. You wouldn't . . ." The words died stillborn as a rock crashed against his head and he plunged into blackness.

Runs Toward edged into consciousness in bits and pieces. First came the splitting pain of his headache, the white light of the sun that poked through slitted eyelids and into his brain. Next came the chafing of rough rope against his wrists, the realization that he was tied, hands behind his back. He couldn't move, and for a moment he felt as though he couldn't breathe.

He opened his eyes wider. As his pupils shrank, the world took on boundaries. First, blinding light and black, then the silhouette of the cottonwood tree. Runs Toward was lying beneath a wide-spreading limb—and just as that realization ambled into his consciousness, a rope sailed over the limb. A wide loop dropped toward him.

The young Cree rolled over on to his belly and drew his knees beneath him in a fetal position. He struggled to rise, expecting to see his executioners ringing the tree. But there was only the boy, Jimmy, shaking the rope free of a rough spot on the limb, willing it to drop nearer his captive.

Runs Toward scrambled to pull himself to his feet, and Jimmy picked up the rifle propped against the tree. "She's loaded," he said. "I took some of your shells. That's all. You give me any trouble, now, and I'll do more than put a knot on your head."

Runs Toward settled back on his haunches. "What do you mean to do?"

"Just hoist you up onto your horse. I'll tie up your reins and you can guide her with your knees. First place you come to can cut you loose."

Runs Toward shook his head. "You don't have to hoist me on my horse."

"How're you going to climb up without using your hands?"

"I'm not."

Jimmy cocked his head, his mind exploring ways to step astride a horse without using hands. He came up blank, so he went back to work, shaking the rope again. The rope pulled free of the rough spot, and the loop fell, curling toward the ground.

"I'm going to slip this under your arms, take a dally on your horse's saddle horn and hoist you up high enough for your horse to get under you. Rosie and I will hold the rope until you get mounted, and then you can leave."

Jimmy looked Runs Toward full in the eyes. "Sorry about taking your shells. I'll make it good when my pa gets back."

"Where is your pa?"

Jimmy stared suspiciously at him. "He'll be back any-time now."

Runs Toward's eyes swept around the camp. He wanted to run, but he knew he couldn't. He would stay here just a little while, give these people a hand. He would run at the first sign of riders, leave this family and this tree in his dust. But he couldn't leave a woman and two children in trouble. He couldn't do that any more than Eli Gilfeather could have left him to die on the Musselshell.

"Maybe I can pitch in a little," Runs Toward said.

Jimmy bristled.

"We're getting along just fine. We don't need anyone's help."

"You would be doing me a big favor if you let me stay awhile. I'm supposed to meet some people here in a couple of days. If they aren't here by then, I'll move along."

Jimmy cocked his head. One eye squeezed almost shut as he considered the request. "Water's worth something."

"How much?"

"Maybe . . . maybe a bullet a day, and I'd get to keep the ten I already have?"

"Fair enough. I can spread my bedroll under the tree?"

Jimmy shook his head and said, "Don't want no red Indian sleeping next to me."

"What if I give you my rifle each night?"

Jimmy nodded. "I guess so."

"Would you untie me now? Time enough yet to go hunting."

"Hunt horseback?"

"Horseback."

"I get the saddle?"

"All right. You get the saddle and I ride bareback."

Jimmy stared at Runs Toward, curious now that he felt more comfortable around the young man. "What did you say they call you?"

"My name is Runs Toward."
"Funny name."
"Not so funny to me."
Jimmy nodded.

Tolkien's Chinese cook poked his head through the bunkhouse door and told Eli, "Mr Tor-keen say I bring you."

The cook's remark was greeted by silence. Tolkien didn't
call people to tell them how much he appreciated their
work. A trip out back, the cowhands had come to call it. If
a cowhand took a trip out back, he was no longer welcome
at the Trident.

Eli licked his lips. Did the old man know about Stringer
Jack, about Eli's meetings with the Musselshell rustler? Gilfeather knelt in deference to his sore back and lifted the
lid of the trunk at the foot of his bed. Inside were the tools
of his trade: fence pliers, hoof clippers, a shoeing hammer,
leather punch, gloves in various states of disrepair.

He always knelt at the trunk before beginning his day's
work. A man needed the right tools to do the job assigned
him. But what tools should a man take on a trip out back?
How could he equip himself to hear that he would cowboy
no more for the Trident—or, by God, any other ranch in
the territory?

The other men in the bunkhouse stared at him, wondering what he had done—or not done. Had they been in-
volved? Would they be the next to take a trip out back?

When Gilfeather felt the eyes on his back and turned
to see, everyone studied the rough bunkhouse floor, each
feigning a lack of interest.

For five years he had worked for the Trident, longer
than he had ever worked anywhere. Maybe too long.

At the Trident, Gilfeather had come to realize his mortality. He had long known death. Death lay in ambush at
every badger hole, awaiting a galloping horse. Death rode
the bitter winds of a killer blizzard, sucking the warmth

and life from anyone it found. Death accompanied the man with shifty eyes and a boot knife into a small-town saloon.

Eli had buried dozens of cowboys, wondering at their vulnerability and his own invincibility. But lately he had begun to read the portent of his own mortality in the scratchy, dim mirrors hanging above the row of washbasins. His hair was graying; his skin was burnt dry as parchment. Eli's body was still tough, shaped by long hours and hard work, but he was almost forty years old, damn near ancient for a cowboy. He couldn't imagine enduring the tough broncs and the cold mornings much longer, and he couldn't imagine doing anything else.

He had taken to putting all of his thirty-dollar monthly pay into a coffee can, keeping only enough to buy tobacco. He wanted a place for himself and Runs Toward. Nothing big; they didn't need much, just a cabin and a creek and a few hundred head of cattle, just a place where it didn't matter if one cowboy was past his prime and another's skin was too dark.

The coffee can had been long filling with bills and coins, but even after years of frugality the ranch hadn't amounted to much more than a notion.

All his life, he had lived on the edge, but always he toed the line on honesty. He spoke the truth as well as he knew it, paid his debts, and stayed on the right side of the law.

But old age was on the horizon now, like the white line of a winter blizzard. He couldn't go into that storm without a little extra to get him and Runs Toward through it. Only after he stared that reality full in the eyes did Eli Gilfeather make his deal with the devil.

As he sold information to the rustlers, the coffee can filled. He had almost enough for a cabin and breeding stock. By the end of the summer, he could have put together a pack string and pointed them north toward Canada to meet Runs Toward.

He could have done that—if Mr. Tolkien hadn't summoned him out back.

Eli stepped into a warm Montana evening. The last tints of a glorious sunset colored the sky to the west. A few stars were becoming visible. The air was redolent with horse apples. The cowboy had been around the odor so long he barely noticed it. His clothing, his sweat, his skin smelled of horses. Only on rare trips to town for a bath at the barbershop and the purchase of clothing fresh and clean from the store did he completely escape the aroma.

A horse whickered from the corral. Probably the paint, more pet than working horse. Tolkien rode the mare only occasionally, currying her himself and making sure she had more than her share of oats.

Eli had wondered more than once at the strange relationship between the gruff cattleman and the mare. It seemed sometimes that the mare nurtured a soft place somewhere inside the old grizzly, buried so deep no human ever saw it.

Eli thumped across the porch, noticing that his palms were damp with sweat. He wiped them on the legs of his pants and stepped up to the door.

"Come in," Tolkien growled.

The old man was perched in a ladder-back chair behind his desk. He stared at Eli, eyes black as a coal and cold as a February night. He was at least two decades older than Eli—his skin was brown as a worn pair of gloves and seemed stretched too thin, as if meant for a man a size or two smaller. The rancher had been rendered by the heat of Montana's summers and the cold of her winters, reduced to a rock-hard core with no more give to it than a granite peak.

The room was spare, to fit the man. The walls were hung with halters and ropes and lanterns. One chair, a table, and a rough cot shared a corner of the room with a black, big-bellied stove that seemed to rise from a pile of wood stacked on the floor beside it. No pictures hung on the wall. No books graced the desk or tabletop. The room held only those things necessary for the continued operation of the Trident ranch.

"Shut the damn door, Mr. Gilfeather. I have no great love for sleeping with mosquitoes and flies."

"Yeah, I don't like that either. I remember one time up on the Milk River. Those mosquitoes were so—"

The old man's eyes squinted and the muscles in his jaw clenched. "Didn't invite you here to listen to your recollections, Mr. Gilfeather."

"No, sir."

"I suppose you're ready for your trip out back."

Eli's brow wrinkled.

"You don't think I know what you boys say about me?" A flicker of smile crossed the old man's face and then vanished. "Surprised you didn't leave after the Injun did." (It was a mark of upbringing that Tolkien called all of his cowboys mister. It was a mark of his battles with Indian tribes that he always called Runs Toward "Injun.")

"Be joining up with him later."

"After you put together enough money to buy a ranch of your own?"

Again Eli's forehead wrinkled.

In response to the unasked question, Tolkien said: "Every cowboy wants his own ranch. They all think I have it easy, sitting in this cabin giving orders. Well, it isn't easy, Mr. Gilfeather. Drought, range fires, killer blizzards: You boys get paid. It isn't that way with me. My income is based on how fat the steers are when I can load them in a train car bound for a Chicago slaughterhouse. Right now, I'm not making very much money, Mr. Gilfeather." The old man's face contorted as though he had just bitten a sour lemon. "Rustlers are putting my profit in their pockets."

Eli dropped his head and scratched the back of his neck.

"Do you know what it says in the Bible about stealing, Mr. Gilfeather?"

"Uh . . . says you shouldn't do it."

"The Bible says that to steal is a sin. An English gentleman by the name of Edmund Burke once said that 'the only thing necessary for the triump of evil is for good men to do nothing.' Cattlemen are finished with doing nothing, Mr. Gilfeather. We have taken it upon ourselves to stamp out sin.

"We will free this country of the sinful ways of some of its residents. We intend to rid this country of all rustlers. We intend that rustlers will know the penalty for stealing cattle in this territory. That's the reason we hanged that . . . miscreant we found on a Trident horse."

"Mr. Tolkien, I don't think that was a Trident horse. I know Trident stock as well as anyone, and I've never seen that—"

Tolkien's face glowed red and he spoke through clenched teeth. "Mr Gilfeather! I did not ask you to come here to argue with me! Who do you think you are?"

Eli's back straightened. "I'll tell you who I am, Mr. Tolkien. I'm the one who risked my life to pull some of your precious cows out of snowdrifts, and to fight those range fires that almost wiped out half your ranch. I've run my life into the ground so you can grub a few extra dollars off a range that you have no more right to than I do.

"That's who I am, Mr. Tolkien. I'm the one at the bottom of the heap, right under your boot heel."

When Eli glared into the old man's face, the lower half of Tolkien's face was twisting into a sardonic smile.

"So that's it," Tolkien said.

"What do you mean?" The coldness of the old man's smile drained Eli's anger and replaced it with fear.

"*That's* what makes a man like you a thief."

Eli's eyes squinted into slits. "I don't take kindly to being called a thief."

"I don't take kindly to having people who put their boots under my table steal from me." The old man leaned across the table and said, "The minute that savage friend of yours left this place, I knew it was you. I can't prove it—yet. If I could, I'd hang you right now and leave you like a skinned coyote to scare those damn rustlers away.

"I can't prove it, and I can't trust you, so I'm taking you with me on a little expedition to rid this country of thieves. You will stick to me like pine pitch, Mr. Gilfeather. Every time we come up to a bunch a rustlers, you're going to worry that one of them will spill the beans on you to save his own miserable neck. And as soon as one of them does, I'm going to hang you, Mr. Gilfeather. I'll put the rope around your neck myself and I'll watch you choke."

CHAPTER 5

THEY DRIFTED INTO the ranch, silent, as tumbleweeds, gathering in little knots. The silence was broken only by whispered conversations as one or another of the cowboys rolled a cigarette or turned to tie his duster behind his saddle.

Eli Gilfeather exchanged barely perceptible nods with some of the men, the kind of nods an auctioneer watched for when he was playing to a bunch of close-mouthed cowboys. Gilfeather had worked with many of the riders on roundups and brandings where the ranches sifted through the wild stock to determine which calves were their own. Mostly good men.

This day was an adventure that would break the boredom of their lives, like the monthly hooraws in the nearest saloon. Danger played the edges of the crowd, setting nerve ends tingling. Horses sensed their riders' nervousness and danced, bits jangling.

The men were well armed because they expected the rustlers to fight for their lives, preferring a bullet to a rope. Each man gathered at the Trident ranch knew that he could be killed in the fight, and that straightened his back a bit. Even sitting astride their horses, the men seemed to be strutting.

Eli wondered for a moment if any of the others were suspected rustlers, as he was. His eyes searched theirs, watching for any indication that others shared his predicament. But the cowhands had carved their faces into emotionless masks, and Gilfeather could read no guilt on them.

The Chinese cook appeared in the chilly morning air, blue enameled coffee pot steaming in his hand, offering the black liquid to take the chill from cowboy bones, to clear their minds for the task at hand. He made the rounds, pot clinking against tin cups.

The coffee helped pull them together. Conversation poked into the gathering. Some low chuckles accompanied stories of past roundups and past cowboys: "Remember that time that Jerry Wing tried to fork that mean, black, balded-faced old bronc. I swear that man turned three full somersaults before he hit the dirt. Stood up, shook the dust off, and said, 'Well, I'll bet that bronc won't try *that* again.' "

The door to the ranch house opened, and a man in a dark wool vest and long wool coat stepped out. Back straight as a corral post and just as stiff, he strode toward the men, Tolkien following a respectful distance behind.

Whispers rippled through the men. "Zebediah Harkins . . . The association's in this, all right . . ." And then silence, in the presence of the most powerful men in Montana.

Most men would have climbed atop a wagon seat to command the cowboys' attention. This man stood in a yard spattered with horse apples and cattle manure, and still the men on horseback felt they were looking up at him. He stroked his chest-length beard at his chin and when the group was in total silence, he began to speak.

"We are gathered here today in the name of justice. No one can really understand the value of that esteemed word until they have been forced by circumstance to do without it. The law simply cannot enforce its will against the undesirable elements of society in this vast territory. So justice, gentlemen, is left to us.

"We are setting out on an historic task. We will make this territory safe. We will exact justice from those whose only sense of morality is their all-consuming greed. We will make this state safe, and just, once again.

"Because justice and law are not always partners, our actions will be questioned by some. Therefore, to protect ourselves, we must each swear an oath of silence. What occurs today and subsequently must never be spoken of outside this circle. If any of you wish to leave this endeavor, do so now. No other opportunity will present itself, because once we have left this ranch, you are in for the duration."

His stern, dark eyes probed the ring of men.

"Have we reached an understanding, then?"

The cowboys nodded.

"Good. We'll ride with the blessing of the decent people of this territory to rid Montana of this ugly business."

Runs Toward shifted in his bedroll to avoid the knot or rock that had plagued him all night, poking into his sleep. His eyes seemed welded shut. It must be early, very early.

He forced his lids open and peeked into the day as the sun was just beginning to edge into the world. The tree above him was still in darkness, its leaves rustling in a breeze Runs Toward couldn't feel down on the ground.

A distant memory came to him. The acrid taste of leaves. He had tasted them when he was a child, when he used to rub his tongue against many things, to feel the rough bark of the cottonwood or the softness of his mother's hair.

His mind drifted between sleep and wakefulness, as the day was drifting now from dark to light. The horses, sensing that he was awake, snuffled and stamped their feet in greeting. He called to them with his mind, told them what great creatures they were and how pleased he was with them. One of the horses whickered in response.

Runs Toward lay in the warmth of his blanket, stretching his body and his mind to meet the day. False dawn had come to the prairie, and the branches of the tree were taking on definition in the growing light.

He rolled over on his back, his eyes looking straight up

into the faintly brightening sky through the tree's branches. Runs Toward could feel life in the tree, palpable as the tree's rough gray bark, trace it in the sap rising in exaltation to greet the sun. He could feel death, too, like the constriction of a rope choking off life.

Runs Toward lifted his head to stare toward the east and the coming sun. Only a faint gray presaged its coming. It was too dark still to read his pocket watch, but he guessed that the time was three, or perhaps three-thirty. Early yet, but not too early to begin a day.

One of the horses whickered again, anxious to be rid of its picket, to sip some cool, clear water from the spring.

Runs Toward rolled over onto his belly and pushed himself into a sitting position. Once free of his bedroll, he felt the chill of the morning air. He shivered, anxious to slip into the flannel shirt he kept under the covers with him so it would be warm in the morning. But the shirt and his woolen trousers had slipped from the bedroll with his tossing during the night.

He had faced his executioners again last night in his dream. That thought rippled down his back, and he shivered again as he shook his clothing to rid it of any hunting spiders that had sought warmth there in the cool June night.

The young Cree looked toward the dugout, a low shape, blacker than the tree in shadow, blacker than the sun was light. It was then that he saw shadow. Jimmy Wilder had slept outside, sitting in the darkness, with his rifle across his lap.

The boy stood and whispered to Runs Toward, "You're wasting the best part of the day. It's time to go hunting."

Jimmy Wilders rode behind and a little to the right of Runs Toward. That kept the muzzle of the rifle only inches from the Cree's back.

Occasionally, the boy's eyes flickered to a promising

patch of juniper, or a swale that might hold an antelope, but mostly Jimmy kept his attention focused on the Cree. The young man rode easily on the horse, and Jimmy envied him that. Over the past six weeks, the boy had spent so much time walking that he had marveled when first climbing astride Runs Toward's pack gelding. How strange to be moving without effort!

But now, the saddle seemed hard as a rock. Each step of the horse sent a jolt through the boy that made his legs ache. He wondered for a moment how long it would be before he felt comfortable again astride a horse. He hoped the Cree and his horses would be gone by then.

False dawn was full now, and it would only be moments before the sun rose in the East. False dawn was the best time to hunt: Deer and antelope nibbled still at dew-wet grasses. With the soft light of morning, predators were seeking their dens, carrying home to their young the bounty of the hunt. So the animals that ranged the plains converting grass and browse into meat for wolves and coyotes felt a little easier.

On most mornings, Jimmy would be straining to hear the thump of a running rabbit, the swish of branches as a deer broke loose of a patch of junipers. He would be testing the air for the musky scent of deer.

Most mornings, Jimmy Wilder would be as much a part of the prairie as the deer and antelope, sage and juniper. But today, he was Jimmy Wilder, guardian of his mother and sister. His attention was split, as he watched for wild game while keeping an eye on the Indian.

Runs Toward seemed completely at ease. Jimmy wondered at that. In the half hour of their ride, Jimmy's eyes had been boring into Runs Toward's back. Surely, he felt that.

But Runs Toward seemed not to notice the boy behind him. He rode across the prairie, watching from the corner of his eyes for the flicker of movement that would mean game. His eyes roved hillsides and horizons, watching for an ear defined in shadow, for the glint of light reflecting from an antler or horn.

Suddenly he stopped, motioning for Jimmy to come up. Jimmy hesitated and then rode up beside him, but about ten feet away. Runs Toward shook his head. "You've got to decide if you're hunting me or meat, Jimmy."

"What do you mean?" The words came louder than they should have, and challenging.

"I mean that you just rode past a bunch of antelope and you didn't even notice them."

Jimmy jerked around in his saddle. "Where?"

"Hush," Runs Toward hissed. "And sit still or you'll spook them. They're about a mile to the right, just under the crest of that hill. The only one that you can see is the sentry, but I caught the flash of the sun off the horns of one on the slope below."

Jimmy's eyes searched the hillside. There! A flash of white and yellow. He could see the animal now, no doubt watching them as carefully as they were watching her.

Jimmy eased his face to the right. The prairie lay flat and open as a tabletop between them and the animals. No. A trace of green and shadow marked a coulee. If they could reach the coulee . . . No. No cover. The animals would spook in a minute.

Jimmy turned to face Runs Toward. "What do we do? Make a run at them?"

Runs Toward shook his head. "They'd be out of sight before we covered half the distance."

"It's our best bet." Jimmy reined his horse toward the animals on the far hill.

"Jimmy, you run at the herd, and that's the last we'll see of them."

"Walking away from them won't put meat on the table."

"Walking away doesn't mean you can't come back."

Jimmy cocked his head and stared at his companion.

Runs Toward's hat cast his face in morning shadow and made it seem darker still. Jimmy weighed Runs Toward's words and the glitter of his eyes.

"Indians are supposed to be good hunters."

"Yeah," Runs Toward said. "Indians are."

"All right."

Runs Toward kicked his horse into a walk. They rode for nearly half a mile in full view of the herd. The sentinel doe watched them go; as they moved away, she stopped to nibble at the grasses and sagebrush at her feet.

The two continued west for nearly a mile, dropping into the first wash they found.

"Tie the gelding to that juniper," Runs Toward whispered. "Take off the bridle and loosen the cinch."

They left the horses seeking grass in the bottom of the wash. The two followed the wash down to the coulee below, stepping carefully over dried juniper limbs washed into the cut by spring rains past.

Runs Toward leaned down and whispered, "We'll follow this coulee back east toward the herd. There's another wash that works its way up just below them. We'll follow that up and be right in the middle of that bunch. We should get one each. That's enough. In this weather, they won't keep long, and we haven't got anything to smoke them with. Take a buck. More meat."

Jimmy's eyes squinted nearly shut. "I'm not taking orders from any red-skinned Indian."

"You want meat?"

Jimmy nodded.

"Then do as I say."

"I'll do as I want."

"If you want meat, you'll do as I say."

"You're not my boss!"

Runs Toward sighed, twisted his neck as though it ached. "No, Jimmy, I'm not your boss. Hunger is your boss, just like it is everyone else's.

"We'll make meat today. We know where the herd is, so there's no need to peek while we're working up on them. The only thing we have to concentrate on is being quiet. Go slow and watch every step. Time doesn't matter. Silence does. Put your feet down soft on the earth and follow the silt wherever you can.

"When we go up the wash, we'll be on our bellies. One sound and that bunch will spook. So we go with no sound. No talk.

"Can you do that, Jimmy?"

Jimmy nodded.

"Good. Today we will send hunger away."

Jimmy's legs were trembling when Runs Toward motioned for the two to stop. For more than a mile, the two had followed the bottom of the coulee, keeping to the dry, silty soil when possible, choosing bare rock when it wasn't so the scrape of rock against rock would not announce their presence.

The strain had been profound. The two had been traveling slowly, placing each foot with care. Once, Runs Toward motioned Jimmy to stop, and they stood poised while a cottontail in a juniper bush decided the two were not so dangerous and hopped slowly off to a safer hiding place.

Jimmy had long since lost any sense of where they were. He thought they had stalked past the herd, but he kept going. They were walking silently in a world inhabited by loose rocks and dry sticks and frightened rabbits.

Jimmy had walked the distance afraid that he would be the one to send a loose rock clattering across stones below, afraid that the sound would send a covey of grouse skyward to signal the hunters' presence.

Runs Toward raised his index fingers to his lips, and Jimmy realized he had been grinding his teeth. Now they locked together, and he shut his eyes in anger at himself. Had the click he heard in the bones of his head carried beyond him? Runs Toward scowled, and Jimmy knew the answer. His eyes closed, and he felt the breath leave him in an imperceptible sigh. All this distance. They had come all this distance, and he probably spooked the antelope by clicking his teeth together.

Runs Toward was pointing up a wash angling steeply up the hill to the north. It was the wash he had marked when he first saw the antelope sentinel and the glint of horns on the hill below. Jimmy couldn't understand how he could recognize it: The wash looked no different from the dozens of others they had passed on their cautious way down the coulee.

The Indian held his index finger to his lips, and Jimmy's face glowed red beneath his deep tan. Jimmy's body ached with silence, with the tension of putting each foot in exactly the right place, praying every step of the way that he wouldn't be the one to spook the herd and leave his family hungry.

Who the heck did that redskin think he was, anyway? No one had asked him to throw in with the Wilders. Runs Toward was on this hunt because Jimmy said he could be, not the other way around.

Jimmy glared at Runs Toward, and the Cree's brow knitted questioningly.

Jimmy pointed at the Cree, and waved him up the wash. The Cree shook his head, but Jimmy stood firm.

Runs Toward shrugged and threw out his hands, palms up. If Jimmy didn't want the first shot, that was all right with him. Runs Toward crouched and started up the wash. Each step was planned, each followed by a long pause as he scoured the rim above him with his eyes. His ears strained for the sound of hooves thumping against the prairie. If the band spooked before they reached the top, the two hunters would have to scramble up, hoping the antelope stopped long enough for one quick shot.

Jimmy followed, stretching his stride a little to put his

feet exactly where Runs Toward's boots marked the soil. The boy's exhaustion disappeared as they approached through the wash. His heart was thumping in his chest, and he was alive to the land around him. Silently they moved, so silently that when a yellowjacket buzzed through the air between them, it sounded like a passing locomotive.

The insect landed on Runs Toward's shirt, near the collar. The young Cree flinched, but the yèllowjacket ignored his host's warning, moving up to explore the exposed skin where the collar met neck. When the wasp's six legs touched Runs Toward's neck, he flinched again, the motion moving his collar up his neck, almost trapping the insect.

Jimmy watched, fascinated as the insect drove its stinger into Runs Toward's neck again and again and again. Then, free of the collar, the wasp flew clumsily into the air and buzzed off in its never-ending search for food. Runs Toward stood still as a statue, and even from where he stood, Jimmy could see knots growing on the Cree's neck. They looked white, as though the pain had transformed itself into color, into a fierce, white-hot ache.

Runs Toward's neck canted to the side, and Jimmy could see the young man's chest heave in a silent sigh. Then Runs Toward moved on and Jimmy followed, one eye on the Cree's footprints and one eye out for the belligerent wasp.

Jimmy's heart was crashing against his chest, not so much with exertion as with excitement. As Runs Toward neared the top, he crouched lower and lower, shedding his hat finally so the antelope would see no sign of him poking into their resting area until his eyes met theirs.

Just below the lip of the wash, Runs Toward settled back on his haunches and motioned for Jimmy to join him. When the boy was crouching beside him, rifle at the ready, Runs Toward began to stand and the boy followed him, the two rising in unison so that they seemed tied together.

The hillside was covered with grass and sage and yucca. Juniper bushes spread their branches and scent over the scene.

Jimmy glared at Runs Toward. "You took us up the wrong wash," he hissed. "I thought Indians were supposed to be good hunters."

Suddenly the hillside exploded in antelope, yellow and white and black. The two were in the middle of the herd, surrounded by confused animals darting about, seeking a common path so they could put their noses into the wind and run from this strange sound and the two creatures in their midst.

Jimmy stood wide-eyed while the animals sprinted around him. Then, he heard the crack of Runs Toward's rifle. One of the animals tumbled and fell twitching on the prairie, and the herd was gone.

Runs Toward leaned down to the boy, scowling.

"I thought I told you to be quiet."

CHAPTER 6

THE VIGILANTES PARADED out of the yard, kicking up dust that blended with the scent of horse and old leather.

Gilfeather held back, letting the horsemen pass him. His turn would come, and he would follow, pressed into duty by Old Man Tolkien's suspicions. The other men nodded as they passed, saluting one another as if they were soldiers on a quest for justice.

Tolkien also let the men pass. He waited until Eli's gelding stepped beside him; then the old man eyed him knowingly. Gilfeather's jaw clamped shut and the two men spurred their horses to the head of the column.

Most of the men assumed Gilfeather must be Tolkien's chosen.

The ascension to foreman or manager of ranches was a mystery. None of the cowboys knew why one man was picked over another. Each thought himself better qualified to manage than the one selected.

They often resented being passed over, showing their indignation in words spoken behind the foreman's back, in sullen stares. Only after a number of years, when the foreman's judgment was proven sound, did they pull him back into their confidence.

The men stared at Gilfeather now, minds sifting through past roundups, trying to remember the special effort, the spark, that caused Tolkien to pick the cowboy as lead bull.

No one suspected that Tolkien had called Gilfeather to the front of the column so he could keep an eye on him.

The old man was riding his pinto. Gilfeather understood Tolkien's affinity for the mare. She was as soft-footed as she was sure. A beautiful black and white animal, she would be almost invisible at a distance, walking through patches of light and shadow in the Missouri River bottom.

Gilfeather took a deep breath of the prairie air. His habit tugged at him, and he reached for the sack of tobacco and papers resting in his shirt pocket.

"You can smoke when we take a break," Tolkien said gruffly.

Gilfeather's eyes jerked around to the old man.

"You're upwind. I don't care for the smell of tobacco."

Gilfeather's eyes squinted shut. "I'll smoke when I damn well please."

"You will smoke when I tell you you can. You will eat, sleep, drink, squat, and smoke when I tell you, Mr. Gilfeather. You will ask my permission before you pass wind."

"Like hell, I will."

"Like hell, you won't."

The old man's face swung toward Gilfeather. His eyes were squinted into slits, his voice was a whisper squeezed between gritted teeth. "I haven't told the other men about my suspicions, Mr. Gilfeather, but if you give me any trouble at all, I will. Then everyone will be watching you, not just me. How do you think you'll fare, a suspected rustler riding along with a bunch of vigilantes?"

"You beady-eyed bastard," Gilfeather hissed. He jerked his tobacco and papers from his pocket and tossed them out on the prairie. "You are one sorry excuse for a human being!"

A smile flickered across the old man's face. "You say what you think. I've always appreciated honest talk, Mr. Gilfeather. I've always respected honesty. I guess that's the reason I rank you just a little lower than the belly of a rattlesnake."

"You son of a bitch."

"Cursing is the last resort of the ignorant, Mr. Gilfeather. You are constantly confirming my assessment of yourself."

The horse was stretching, legs reaching for a speed it had never before achieved. Each time the hooves struck the earth, puffs of dust arose like fires struck from steel-shoed feet.

Archie McDonald, scout to the stranglers, raced frantically toward them. The band of men waited, determination and trepidation flickering across their faces. The time for talk was finished. If McDonald had found a large band of rustlers, the battle would begin. Some rustlers and some stranglers were likely to die in the fracas.

If only one rustler had been spotted, they would run him to ground. One of the men would tie a noose and slip it over the thief's neck. Another would slap the rustler's mount, sending the rustler to the gates of hell, as everyone watched.

McDonald jerked back his reins and his horse nearly sat down on her haunches in her attempt to do her master's bidding. McDonald spoke between rasping, sucking breaths, as spent as his horse.

"One man . . . beautiful horse . . . sneaking slow . . . guilty as . . . a coyote in a chicken coop."

McDonald slumped on his horse, sucking air into his lungs.

Tolkien waited until McDonald regained his breath and asked, so casually he might be asking about the weather, "Where?"

"Big coulee up ahead. He's sneaking along a dry cut in the bottom. Stopping every so often to look behind. He's riding a long-legged gray, looks Arabian. Can't be his horse. I'd stake my life on it."

Tolkien's voice was little more than a whisper, "How do we do it?"

McDonald stepped off his mare and loosened her cinch.

He stared at Tolkien for a moment before replying. "Coulee swings north in a big loop. Ride straight east and find a way down off the rim—he'll sneak right into you. If you get rimmed, you'll still have a decent shot. Course, you might hit the horse."

"I sure as hell don't want to kill someone's Arabian," Tolkien said.

"I could take two or three men with me," McDonald said, "and follow his tracks. We'd have him penned in for sure. Could be that if he knew he didn't have a chance, he might step down."

Tolkien nodded. *That's the ticket,* the old man thought. *Get him penned in, front and back.*

"Sneaky bastard." Tolkien spoke with perverse admiration.

The rustler was almost invisible as he rode through the cut in the bottom of the coulee, noticed only when his soft tan hat poked over the edge of the cut or when the Arabian edged up a sidehill to avoid an abrupt drop in the cut's bottom.

Tolkien and Gilfeather hid behind a juniper bush, watching the horseman steal toward them.

"Something to be said for a man who does this job well, even if his job is rustling. Would you agree with that, Mr. Gilfeather? Are you a good rustler?"

Eli's teeth gritted shut.

"Cat have your tongue, Mr. Gilfeather?"

"Were I you," Gilfeather muttered, "I would pay closer attention to that rider."

" 'Were I you'? Where did you receive your schooling, Mr. Gilfeather?"

"I picked it up, just like I got everything else in my life. No one has handed me anything, *Mister* Tolkien. I got my schooling wherever I could find it."

"Well, you got your schooling in the wrong place—

somebody should've taught you not to rustle cattle, especially from me."

The coulee, cut over the centuries by spring rains and summer thunderstorms, was wide and covered with bunchgrass, yucca, juniper, and an occasional stand of bull pine. As the waters had coursed back and forth across the coulee, dry ground was left covered with stones and with soft gray soil that turned to dust when it was windy and to gumbo mud during the slightest rain.

The vigilantes had cut across the prairie above to get in front of the rider. They found a break in the rimrocks and followed a rough trail to the bottom of the coulee. They waited now, hidden behind a ridge from the approaching rider.

Tolkien and Gilfeather had climbed the ridge, hiding themselves behind a great rock that had fallen from the rims above.

"There!" Gilfeather said.

Tolkien nodded. He had seen the hat bob for a moment over the edge of the cut.

The horseman paused, turning to survey the trail behind him.

"Somebody's after him," Tolkien said. "Were I,"—Gilfeather bristled at the old man's sneer—". . . the owner of that beautiful damn horse, I'd be after him, too."

Gilfeather remained silent.

"Well," Tolkien said, "we have him. He doesn't know that the cut disappears in another four hundred yards. We'll let him come out in the open and cut him off. By that time, McDonald and his crew should be coming up behind. That horseman had better start saying his prayers."

Tolkien and Gilfeather scuttled back from the bush, dropping down the ridge to the vigilantes waiting below.

The riders came from a draw to the west of his path, but to Ryder Davis, they seemed spawned by the setting sun.

He squinted into the bright light, watching as the horsemen appeared before him, shadows fleshing out as they rode across the coulee.

Seven men were lined across the coulee floor. Each rider's hat was pulled low over his eyes, partially hiding his face. Each rider's rifle was out, butt propped against the rider's hip, muzzle pointing into the setting sun.

Davis considered wheeling the gray and running. The Arabian was fast as the wind, but Davis knew the horse could not outrun a bullet. Still, if he ran he might have a chance. If he stayed he almost certainly would be killed.

Davis wheeled his horse, but before he touched his boots to the Arabian's belly, he saw the four men behind him, rifles out. Seven men in front of him and four behind. Eleven men. Too damn many.

He sighed and reached down to give the gray an appreciative pat on the neck. The stud shook his head in response. Davis climbed down from the saddle, surrendering to these men who were about to kill him. Maybe he could talk them into letting him write a final letter to his mother and father to tell them how he had come to die on the Montana prairie on the first day of July in the year of our Lord 1884.

The line of horsemen moved toward him, horses stepping slowly across the long-grassed bottom of the coulee. Two horsemen pulled ahead of the bunch and rode toward him at a trot, standing in their stirrups to take the shock of the horse's gait with their knees and not their backs.

The two reined to a stop in front of Ryder Davis.

The older one, the one with a face hard enough to strike sparks from steel, stared at Davis and said, "Nice horse."

Davis nodded.

"Yours?"

Davis shook his head.

"Didn't think so," the old man said. "Your firearms, boy."

Davis stared at the old man. There was no give in the old

man's face; no emotion showed on his sun-burnt, leathery visage.

"Isn't the horse enough?" Davis asked, desperation in his voice.

The old man shook his head.

"Can't you let me go?"

The old man shook his head. "Have to hang you, boy."

"Hang me? When did rustlers take to hanging?"

The old man's brow knotted. "Rustlers? Who the hell are you to call us rustlers? We didn't steal that Arabian."

"Neither did I."

A fire, bigger than it needed to be, marked the stranglers' camp in the bottom of the coulee. A poor dinner of beans had been rinsed off tin plates, and the stranglers ringed the fire, drinking coffee and listening to Ryder Davis.

He sat easy among the men, using his face, arms, and hands to add drama as he talked. Davis was a master storyteller, using pauses as well as words to build images, teasing the men with the story until they leaned forward toward the fire so no words would be missed.

". . . So Captain Bodeen said, 'Do you think you can do it, boy?'

"Well, I had an unholy need to ride his horse. Isn't he the most beautiful creature you've ever seen?"

Nods followed Davis's question around the ring.

"On the other hand, I figured that riding a horse like that through the Missouri River country was like signing my own death sentence."

Davis took a deep breath and looked into the fire.

"Well, I was standing there, figuring my chances, and they weren't very good. I was just about to tell the captain, 'Thank you very much, but I still have some living to do,' when his daughter stepped up beside her daddy."

Davis shook his head and stared again into the fire, seeking words there to fit that moment.

"Well, that stallion is about the prettiest horse I've ever seen, but I'll tell you, he doesn't hold a candle to the captain's filly. Violet eyes, she has. Violet as . . . violet as an August sunset. Her hair black and shiny as a raven's wings and her . . ."

Davis sighed. "I'll tell you boys, she smelled like every flower I've ever seen. Her skin was kind of tawny, not from the sun, but because it was natural that way. Like honey, it was, and I wondered how it would . . ."

Davis looked up, startled. He blushed as the men winked at him and elbowed each other.

"Well, hell. I couldn't tell that captain that I was afraid to go, not with that girl hanging on my every word. I would have walked barefoot through a patch of prickly pear just to see her smile."

Davis picked up a stick and stirred the fire. Sparks rose in a column before dying out. Overhead, stars twinkled, perhaps winking at one another as they listened to Davis's story.

"So I stood there with my heart in my mouth and I told that captain that I would be honored to deliver his horse to Lewistown. Honored. And that girl smiled at me, and I figured that I was just about to float away, so light-headed was I.

"She was there the next morning, too, when I rode away. Fresh as a crocus in spring."

Davis's eyes probed the circle of eyes watching him, glints of reflected firelight.

Davis paused, staring into the flames. He was dressed no differently from the other men around the fire; he carried his specialness in his posture, although his face was handsome enough to turn most women's eyes. At that moment each of the men imagined that he was as handsome, as confident as Davis. Each imagined himself to be staring into the eyes of the captain's daughter.

Shorty Williams's voice cracked as he whispered, "What was her name? The captain's daughter?"

Davis shook his head. "I don't know. I never thought to ask."

A collective sigh left the strangers' throats then, each of them painting his own picture of the captain's daughter, each falling in love as Davis had. There would be little sleep in the camp that night as the men's thoughts sought her in the star-studded sky, as they listened for her voice in the whisper of the breeze through the prairie grasses.

"Well, before I left I rode over to her and looked into her eyes and I swear I saw paradise there. Everything disappeared. Fort Benton, a steamboat down on the levee. All the people passing in the street. Just me swimming in her eyes, drowning in those violet pools and happy to go. Then a horsefly nipped the Arabian and he stood up on his hind legs. I almost fell before I remembered where I was.

"I tipped my hat to the captain's daughter and floated out of town. That Arabian is magic, and we were flying. About five miles out, I started seeing rustlers everywhere. All I could think about was that that horse was as pretty to horse thieves as that captain's daughter was to me.

"So I set to thinking about what I should have thought about earlier: How the hell was I going to live through this trip? I figured that Arabian could outrun any four-legged critter we were likely to come across so I rode out in the open toward Square Butte.

"Well, I wasn't the first man the captain had asked to ferry his horse across that prairie, and you know that those rustlers have ears everywhere."

The men nodded. Yes, sir—they knew about the rustlers' ears.

"So I figured that instead of heading toward Square Butte like I was, that I'd swing a little above the Breaks and head west just north of the Judith Mountains and into Lewistown. Now, that's rustler country, all right, but the rustlers from Fort Benton would be out looking for me around Square Butte, or maybe south along Cowboy Steele Creek. I figured I would avoid the ones I knew were waiting and keep my fingers crossed on the others."

The ring of men considered the strategy for a moment, their nods declaring it valid.

"I was traveling really slow, walking part of the time. No way they would run me down, not on that Arabian, not unless they boxed me in on the bottom of a coulee, the way you fellows did."

Chuckles rumbled around the fire.

"Anyhow, one night I was leading the gray into the dark, thinking that I would make a cold camp. Didn't want a campfire shining like a beacon for rustlers. The night was black as pitch, and I was stumbling along when I stepped down into this swale. There, ahead of me, I could see light glowing around the edges of a door. I figured it must be a dugout—no windows or anything. So I stepped up to it and rapped.

"I could hear sounds inside, but no one answered, so I rapped again. Then I heard this voice off to my right, more growl than welcome. Sounded like he was behind a big bull pine I could see against the stars, but I couldn't see him. I realized that about the same time I realized that I was outlined by the light coming through the door. So I stood really still.

"He asked me what I was doing, and I told him looking for a place to spend the night. He asked me what my name was and whose horse I was riding. I told him, and he whistled, and that big door, big enough to be a barn, creaked open.

"I was blinking against the light and somebody inside said to come in and bring my horse with me.

"Well, it was a dugout, all right. Biggest damn dugout I've ever seen. Looked like somebody had found one of those places where a huge, round boulder has broken out from a ledge, leaving a hole that looks like some giant pressed a teacup into the rock and then it fills in on the bottom and front."

Davis stopped, staring at his listeners. "You've all seen those. Like as not you'll find smoke on the walls where some Indians have spent time there."

His listeners nodded. Davis nodded, too, and then he continued. "Well, this was the biggest one I've ever seen. And somebody had filled in the front with rocks and set a door in the center of it."

Davis stirred the fire again. Then he stood, stepping around the fire to take the blue enamel coffeepot by the bail. He poured himself a cup and held the pot up, offering it to his audience. A couple of tin cups poked into the campfire's light, and he filled them, setting the pot back on the flat rock near the fire when he finished. He stretched a little then, working the kinks from his legs before settling again to his rock by the fire.

"I told you it was the biggest dugout I've ever seen. There were eleven men and forty horses in that dugout, and I suspect they could have squeezed another half dozen in there before the horses started to get spooky.

"They were a tough bunch. I'll tell you one thing, I'd never walk into a bar that had a bunch like that in it. They had eyes hard as obsidian, and souls to match.

"Wasn't much I could do, though. I was there and there wasn't any way to get out unless they said I could leave." Davis shook his head. "Forty horses.

"Well, I told them who I was and what I was doing. They thought anyone named Ryder ought to be a rider, and they laughed about that. That softened them up a little, all of them except one old boy they called Kid.

"He couldn't take his eyes off the gray, kept shaking his head and running his hands over the horse. He knew a great horse when he saw one, and I could tell he wanted him for his own. Hell, he even carried water to the stud.

"I could tell they *all* wanted that horse. But the thing of it was, they couldn't all have him. So it was either fight over him or leave him to me.

"Well, there I was in the middle of some of the orneriest-looking men I've ever seen. Wasn't a one of them that wouldn't have ambushed me to get his hands on that horse. But if one of them put a bullet in me and took the horse, someone else would likely put a bullet in *him* and do the same thing.

"There I was in this huge dugout, kerosene lanterns lighting it in yellow, long shadows playing across the walls when one of the horses moved, and even in that light I could see those thoughts percolating through those rustlers' heads. They all wanted that horse so bad they could taste it, but they didn't dare take him.

"Well, I'll be damned if they didn't decide to let me go on. And after they worked that out, they were fairly decent people. They broke out a bottle of whisky, and we all had a drink and then another and then . . . well. Hell, you all know how that goes."

Ryder tossed another stick on the fire and waited until he cold feel the men awaiting his next words.

"Well, in the morning I got up quiet as I could, and saddled the gray, trying not to wake any of them. But when I stepped out, one of them was already standing guard out by that bull pine. He said, 'So long,' and I did, too, and I climbed aboard the gray, expecting any minute that he might shoot me right off that horse.

"The gray had taken only a few steps when I heard him say, 'Ryder,' and the hairs went up on the back of my neck. 'You'd best be watching your backside. The Kid wants your horse.'

" 'Not my horse,' I said.

" 'Not for long,' he said.

"Well, I managed to outrun them. But I've been watching my back trail ever since. That's the reason I thought you were rustlers."

Old man Tolkien's raspy voice grated into the circle. "Think you could find that dugout again?"

Davis shook his head. "Came up on it in the dark. Don't have any idea where it is. It would be pretty tough to find, hidden the way it is against the rimrock. Way I figure it, I'd a lot rather not see it again."

"Well," the old man said, "you can ride with us for a while. Suppose you'll be following the Judith into Lewistown."

Davis nodded. "Figure to be there in time for the Fourth of July hooraw."

"Could be we'll see you there."

Davis scuffed his feet in the dust beside the campfire. "Don't mean to be nosy, but just what is it you folks are doing out here?"

The faces around the fire turned toward Tolkien. "Just looking for strays," the old man said.

"Yeah, well, this stray is going to turn in. Be a real relief to catch some shut-eye without wondering if the Kid's out there just waiting for me to drift off."

"We'll be watching," the old man said.

Davis nodded. He was betting on that.

CHAPTER 7

THE BOY AND his sister spent the early morning searching the prairie for buffalo chips. They gathered as many as they could and placed them in a burlap sack.

Jimmy stopped in the shade of the cottonwood to rub the sweat off his forehead with his shirtsleeve. He set the burlap sack down at his feet. "This ought to do it."

Rosie staggered into camp after him. The sweat on her face had cut furrows through the dirt. Usually talkative, she staggered over to the cottonwood's trunk and dropped to the grass, propping her back against the tree.

Jimmy grasped the bottom of the sack, lifting it so the contents tumbled out on the grass. Runs Toward was tending a fire to heat some water.

One of the chips landed on its edge and rolled, falling flat fifteen feet away. Jimmy, languid in the heat, stepped through the shade of the tree, hesitating before stepping into the full light of the sun where the chip lay, bottom side up. He was too tired to bend over to pick up even one more buffalo chip, so he scuffed the chip to the pile with the toe of his shoe.

"Not going again," Rosie said. "Can't make me." Her independence declared, she dropped her head back against the trunk. Only her eyes moved.

"This should do it," Runs Toward said, tossing a couple of chips on the fire. He reached in to test the water warming in the tub propped up on rocks over the fire. "Sure you have all your clothes out here?"

"Must have walked ten miles," Jimmy said.

"I walked forever," Rosie agreed.

"Didn't know we had picked the prairie around here so clean," Jimmy said.

"We picked up every chip we saw, except in the cactus," Rosie added.

"You two did a good job," Runs Toward said. "Now, are you sure these are all the clothes you have?"

Jimmy nodded, almost imperceptibly.

Runs Toward tossed a blanket at each of the children.

"Cover yourselves and strip. We'll wash everything."

Rosie disappeared beneath the blanket. The blanket bent and stood, weaving blindly. Arms protruded beneath the heavy wool as she felt her way back to the tree and dropped her clothing in a heap on the grass.

Jimmy made a tent of his blanket. Inside it he shed his clothes, a skinny hand periodically reaching out with an article of clothing pinched between thumb and forefinger. Each was taken by Runs Toward, held at arm's length.

The Cree scooped up Rosie's clothing and dropped her dress, undergarments, and stockings into water steaming in one of the two tubs. He rinsed his hands in the hot water and wiped them on his pants.

"Jimmy, what about your mother's clothes?"

The boy leaned against the tree with weariness. He tied two corners of the blanket over his shoulders and looped his belt around his middle. Then he rolled himself forward to his knees and stood. He tiptoed to the dugout, stepping carefully to avoid cactus and sharp rocks and greasewood, returning a moment later with some dresses.

"These were piled on the floor," he said.

"What is your mother doing?"

"Sitting at the table. That's about all she does. Just sits at the table."

"Why don't you get her? Bring her out here."

"I can't. I don't think she ever will come out. Not till Pa comes home."

"Jimmy, she has to leave that dugout. It isn't healthy for

her to sit in there every day. The dugout's like a tomb, and if we don't bring her out, she'll bury herself in there."

The boy's reply was little more than a whisper. "I think she already has."

"Go get her, Jimmy. Put her chair under the tree. We have to help her."

Jimmy sagged perceptibly within his blanket, but he picked his way back to the dugout. He appeared a moment later at the dugout's door, dragging the chair with one hand and his mother with the other.

Sarah Wilder, hair stringy and dress stained, balked at the door. The light seemed to pierce her eyes, her soul, and she struggled against it, struggled to remain in the darkness.

Jimmy released the chair, which fell almost soundlessly against the dirt floor. The boy grasped his mother's hand in both of his then, and tugged her. Her eyes widened in terror, and she bent, bracing her legs at the doorway, fighting to remain in the darkness, the safety, of the dugout.

Jimmy tugged harder. The two were deadlocked in the struggle, and then Rosie appeared, the blanket draped around her shoulders and dragging on the ground behind her.

"Come on, Mommy," she said, taking her mother's hand. The word's pierced Sarah Wilder's consciousness, and a perplexed expression crossed her face as though she were aware for the first time of where she was, what was happening.

That look remained on her face as she followed her little girl to the tree, her eyes blinking at the sunlight.

"You better bring the chair," Rosie said, "so Mommy will have a place to sit."

Jimmy followed, dragging the chair through the grass, bumping against rocks half hidden in the prairie soil. He set the chair on flat sandstone so the legs wouldn't sink in the soft, cool soil beneath the tree. Rosie helped her mother sit down, talking to her as though she were a doll or an imaginary playmate attending a tea party.

The three Wilderses sat, then, with their backs to the cottonwood, while Runs Toward scrubbed their clothing against a washboard thrust into a steaming tub. Whenever the water grew too hot for his touch, he took a bucket of water from the steaming tub and replaced it with cool water from the spring. In that way, the dirt from the clothing was returned to its source.

Runs Toward spent hours hunched over the tub. His hands were wrinkled, and the muscles of his neck and shoulders screamed their exhaustion. He rotated his head, letting it fall toward his chest—shoulder—back—shoulder—chest, and then pulled up his shoulders so the muscles at his neck knotted and braced his head.

After he had draped the last garment, Jimmy's tattered but clean shirt, on the rope strung from a low-hanging limb to the wagon he dried his hands on two large towels he had asked Jimmy to get for him. The summer air was warm and dry and the clean clothing was taking on the scent of the sun.

"Now it's your turn," he said, turning to Jimmy and Rosie.

"You already washed everything," Jimmy said.

"Everything but you two."

"Not me," Jimmy said. "I washed just this morning."

"When was the last time you took a bath?"

Jimmy's forehead knotted. "Not so long."

"You're long overdue. Take it from somebody who's ridden downwind from you."

"I'll go," Rosie said.

"She always gets the clean water."

"We'll put some fresh in after she finishes," Runs Toward said. "Jimmy, you and I will stand sentry to be sure that no one rides up and surprises Rosie."

The two stepped out to the edge of the tree's shade and stared across the sun-drenched prairie. Rosie yelped. "It's hot. Too hot."

"Cover yourself up, Rosie, and I'll bring you some cold water."

Runs Toward waited a moment or two and then carried a bucket of water from the spring to the tub. He felt the heated water with his hand.

"Just a half bucket more and it should be perfect," he said.

When Runs Toward returned to his sentinel's post with Jimmy, backs to the fire, Rosie declared, "Just right. Feels good, Jimmy. Who's going to wash my hair?"

"Who usually washes your hair?" Runs Toward asked the little girl.

"Mommy."

"Ask her."

"Will you wash my hair, Mommy?"

Rosie turned to Runs Toward, "She didn't say anything."

Runs Toward approached Sarah Wilders in her chair as he might have approached a young calf, knowing that the creature would run for its life if he frightened it. He squatted in front of Sarah so that his height would not overpower her. The two sat in silence, he probing her face with his eyes. She seemed oblivious to everything around her, alone in the midst of those most dear to her.

Runs Toward stood slowly so he wouldn't startle her, and offered her his hand. When she didn't take it, he reached down and took hers. His voice was soft, calming when he said, "Rosie, you cover yourself with the towel, except for your back."

Then Runs Toward helped Sarah Wilders to her feet and led her, docile as a lamb, to the tub warming over the fire of buffalo chips.

The young Cree spread one of the heavy towels on the grass and helped Sarah Wilders to kneel on it. She looked in wonder at the bar of soap he placed in her hand. Runs Toward dipped Sarah's hand and soap in the water. He guided her hand in circular motions across Rosie's back, pale as a fish belly under the layer of dirt that had shielded it from the sun.

"That feels good, Mommy."

At the sound of Rosie's voice, Sarah Wilders's hand took on a life of its own, instinctively scrubbing her child's back.

Runs Toward rose, returning to Jimmy's side. The two stood silently, staring across a prairie bleached colorless by the sun, listening to the one-sided conversation behind them.

Hope flickered across Jimmy's face, but he hid it, afraid of being disappointed. He had missed his mother for so long, and had almost given up hope that she would ever come back to them.

Still, he listened to Rosie talking to their mother. He savored the chatter as a thirsty man might savor the last drops of water in a canteen.

"Now my hair, Mommy. Don't forget to wash my hair."

"Careful, Mommy. Don't get soap in my eyes."

"Would you help me get dry, Mommy, and get me some clothes from the line?"

"Don't they smell good, Mommy?"

"Am I your prettiest girl ever, Mommy? You always tell me that I'm your prettiest girl ever."

Runs Toward turned and saw Rosie dressed in a yellow-and-white dress. Her auburn hair, still wet, was slicked back from her face, all brown and freckled and beautiful.

"You look like a flower, Rosie," Runs Toward said.

"Am I the prettiest girl ever?"

"Prettiest ever."

Runs Toward stepped toward the fire and found Sarah Wilders staring in confusion at him.

"Who are you?" she whispered.

"Nothing like a bath to make a person feel better," Runs

Toward said with a smile. "Suppose Jimmy and I were to rig up a little shelter with some blankets under this tree. Wouldn't you like to take a bath, Mrs. Wilders?"

Fear crossed the woman's face and she glanced with longing at the safety of the dugout. He caught her arm as she took her first step toward the darkness. She struggled for a moment—and then stopped, as though the effort had exhausted her.

"Who are you?" she whispered.

"Just a friend. Jimmy, let's rig up a little shelter for your mother so she can take a bath, too. It's a nice day for it."

"No," Sarah moaned, shaking her head, leaning back from the pressure of Runs Toward's hand on her arm. "No. I have to go home now." Her eyes, wide and rolling, sought the safety of the dugout, its cool darkness.

Jimmy stepped up to his mother, his face pale beneath the deep tan, to take his mother's other arm. His voice broke, as though he were trying to speak and swallow at the same time. "Won't be any trouble," he said. "We'll have it ready in no time, Ma. You'll see."

Confusion crossed Sarah's face. "Jimmy? Jimmy? Where have you been? I've been looking all over for you. And Rosie. Where did she go?"

"She's right here, Ma. Just waiting to help you take a bath."

A perplexed expression crossed Sarah's face, and then she saw Jimmy's shrug. "Oh, that would be very nice. Very nice."

Runs Toward and Jimmy hung blankets from ropes strung from the tree. Rosie presided over the filling of the tub with water, determined to bathe her mother as she had been bathed, and Jimmy carried his mother her favorite dress, fresh from the line.

Eli Gilfeather followed a faint deer trail winding its way through a stand of cottonwood and pine Behind him he could hear the measured tread of Old Man Tolkien, and again Gilfeather had the feeling that he was more prey than hunter on this excursion.

The creek was small and shallow, muttering to itself as it dropped past rocks and logs, impediments to its inevitable fall toward the sea.

Gilfeather stopped, leaning down to look under the low-spreading branches of pine trees, watching for bedded deer or the legs of a man waiting in ambush. A cutthroat trout, named for the band of red at the back of its jaw, flashed and swirled in creek water so clear it seemed nothing more than liquefied air. The trout had snatched a passing trout fly. Other trout, green shadows, lay in wait for prey to drift by.

Too bad he hadn't brought his fishing pole with him. Gilfeather's mouth watered at the thought of fresh trout frying in a pan of bacon grease. He turned, and Tolkien nodded. Maybe the old man could read his mind. Or maybe the thought of frying cutthroat watered every man's mouth.

Gilfeather's attention strayed beyond the creek to the wide valley floor. Tall grass and wild daisies outlined boulders worn smooth by ancient glaciers and streams. The meadow was beautiful, a land at peace with itself.

Gilfeather envied the man who had chosen this valley for his cabin. He could spend the rest of his life chasing cutthroat trout in the creek, watching contented cows grazing across the valley floor.

But that thought pulled Gilfeather back to the task at hand. No siree, he didn't envy this man one damn bit. Before long that man would be doing the two-step at the end of a rope. He glanced again at Tolkien. The old man was grinning, grinning like a wolf in a calving pen. That son of a bitch *could* read minds.

Gilfeather's eyes roved again across the trail in front of him. He stepped onto the path again, leaning a little into the hillside, careful so that he would see before he was seen. Maybe that was the only difference between hunter and prey: which was the first to see the other.

The creek swung wide toward the other side of the valley, cutting a "U" in the valley floor. The cabin and corral were set in the bottom of the "U," surrounded on three sides by the creek. A stand of aspen shaded the corral, leaves shaking nervously in a slight breeze.

"Do you see that?" Gilfeather asked.

"Do I see what?"

"The gray. In the corral."

"Yes, I saw him."

"Ryder Davis didn't make it."

The old man shook his head. "No, he didn't."

"Too bad."

"Too bad for him, and too bad for that damn rustler. He's about to reap what he has sown. Mr. Gilfeather, please bring up the rest of the men. Have them tie down anything that might rattle. We don't want our friend to hightail it out of here."

Gilfeather stepped off down the trail, only to be interrupted in mid-step by Tolkien. "Don't run, Mr. Gilfeather. We'd catch you just like we'll catch him. And we'll do the same thing to you that we're going to do to him. You keep that in mind."

"Don't see how I could forget. You remind me every chance you get."

"You don't strike me as a particularly bright man, Mr. Gilfeather. Repetition is necessary."

Gilfeather glared at the old man. That pompous son of a bitch! Gilfeather stalked down the trail, plotting some way to cut through Tolkien's façade.

The horsemen waited in the cover of the trees. They were more than a quarter of a mile from the cabin—perhaps almost half a mile away. Once they stepped into the open meadow, they would be under the muzzle of a rustler's rifle until the vigilantes found their own refuge, at the cabin walls.

The men sat stiff and still in their saddles, eyes probing the sides and doors and windows of the cabin, watching for the telltale glint of sun from the blued barrel of a Winchester lever action, reading the scene for portents of their own death.

They seemed to have stepped into another time. Their hearts beat faster, and the world around them slowed. Flies buzzed through the air as slow and fat as prairie chickens, and the sun seemed not to move at all.

Just at the moment when nerves were beginning to crackle and sputter, just at the moment when the men were ready to ride into that valley of death simply to find relief from the waiting, just at the moment that Tolkien had been waiting for to urge his cavalry into the fray, the horseman appeared.

He was moving slowly up the valley, keeping to cover on the far side. So cautiously did he come that he seemed to be hunting. Tolkien pulled his telescope from his saddlebags and focused on the approaching rider.

"I'll be damned," he said.

All eyes turned to the old man.

"It's Ryder Davis. He's come after his horse. Must have tracked the rustler here, and he's come to get his own. Hell, you boys have been sitting here worrying about taking that cabin, and Davis is aiming to do it all by himself."

Fear is a palpable creature, and Gilfeather could feel it lifting from the men.

"Let's pitch in," Tolkien said, and the men eased forward stepping free of the trees in a long line. Davis stopped, and it seemed for a moment that he might flee, but the old man raised his arm, and Davis seemed to recognize the band. On they came, the young cowboy on the south side of the creek and moving west toward the cabin, and the vigilantes moving almost due south.

Rifles out and the steel-shot butts of the stocks propped against their hips, the cowboys rode toward the first skirmish in their war on rustlers, eyes seeking the puff of blue smoke from the cabin that would mean that a lead pill was on its way from the cabin to cure one of them of life's ills.

But no shots came and they pulled to a line in front of the cabin, Davis joining them seconds later. Tolkien leaned forward in his saddle. "Come on out, Jean LaFontaine. Come on out and meet your Maker."

The cabin door scuffed open, and a man stepped out. His hair was shiny black and woven into two braids tied with rawhide thongs that lay on his heavy wool shirt. His wool pants were held in place by suspenders and tucked into moccasins. The man's eyes were black and set in a craggy, dark face, a map of the lineage of his Métis people, a mix of French trappers and traders and the native peoples of southern Canada.

He stared his visitors full in the face, while cradling a short-barreled shotgun in his left arm, hammers at full cock.

"What do you want?" He spoke with a heavy French accent.

"You," Tolkien said.

"Why?"

"Rustling."

"I see no sheriff."

"We don't need one. You're well known on ranches north of the Missouri. They got your partner just last week, and almost got you. Now we find this young gentleman's gray in your corral."

The Métis's eyes shifted down the line of men to Ryder Davis, who remained silent. LaFontaine's attention was jerked back when the old man spoke again.

"You're not walking away from this, sir. That's the truth of it."

Fear flickered across LaFontaine's face. "You're not going to hang me. So help me God, I'll not choke on the end of a rope, and I'll not go alone. I'll take some of you sons a bitches with me."

LaFontaine's index finger slipped into the shotgun's trigger guard.

"Before you do anything rash, you might consider this." Tolkien edged his horse to the right, and the accused found himself staring into the muzzle of Archie McDonald's rifle.

"Archie, if he makes a move toward us with that shotgun, you wing him," Tolkien said. "We want him alive when we put the rope over his head."

The air thickened with tension, and Ryder Davis seemed to strike sparks as he touched the flank of the bay he was riding and the horse stepped to within fifteen feet of the Métis.

Davis's eyes pinned LaFontaine, and the Métis looked at him, a question reflected in his face.

Davis's voice was soft, unchallenging. "I've been trailing my horse out from Lewistown, where I dropped it off, where you stole it."

The words were explanatory, not accusing. Davis continued, his voice low and soft, soothing. "I met these men on the trail and they saved me from that rustler they call Kid. I'm owing for that. So I don't want them hurt. I don't know what kind of a shot Archie is, but I'm telling you that if you make one move with that shotgun, I'll put a bullet right between your eyes."

LaFontaine's words came just as softly, almost pleading. "Do you really think you can do that?"

"You can bet your life on it."

And LaFontaine did.

He jerked his shotgun toward Davis, and Davis's hand

moved in a blur toward his pistol. The pistol cracked just before the shotgun went *thump* and blew a hole in the cabin's porch. But LaFontaine's shot was triggered by the jerk of not-yet-dead nerves. He fell to the porch, to lie in a spreading pool of his own blood.

"Jee-zuss! Jee-zuss!" The words came from someone astride one of the snorting, wheeling horses fleeing the crash of the weapons and the smell of blood.

But Ryder Davis was already off his horse, standing beside the man he had just killed. His face bleached white and he kneeled, crossing the dead man's hands over his chest and closing his eyes. Then Davis stood, staring down at the man once more before disappearing into the cabin. By the time the vigilantes had quieted their horses—skittish still with the scent of blood—Davis reappeared at the cabin door, carrying a pair of saddlebags.

"He took these when he took the gray," Davis said, returning to his horse and tying the bags behind the saddle. That done, he returned to the porch and stood beside the dead man.

"No sense you waiting," Davis said. "I'll say a few words over him and bury him."

Tolkien shook his head and said, "String him up, boys."

Davis's eyes jerked to the old man. "He's dead."

"Want his friends to see the wages of rustling. People need to know."

"The dead deserve some respect."

"Not dead rustlers. String him up, boys, to that top rafter."

Two men left their horses, gingerly avoiding the dead man's blood as they slipped a noose over his neck. One threw the other end of the rope over the rafter then, jerking LaFontaine into a sitting position. The dead man, bloodied head flopping against his chest, rose then by degrees as the rope jerked him toward the top rafter.

"Hell of a waste of a good rope," one of the men said.

Tolkien nodded. "I'll get you another."

As the two men tugged, a third stepped off his horse, lifting LaFontaine's body as the other two pulled at the rope. With his neck taut against the rafter, LaFontaine's shoes were only about three feet from the ground.

"Well, lookee here," the lifter said. He pulled his sheath knife and cut the thongs lacing the dead man's moccasin to his right foot. Inside was the pouch he had felt and within the pouch were three double eagles.

"It's my lucky day."

Davis walked across the porch, avoiding LaFontaine's body to look up at Tolkien, still mounted on his horse.

"I'll be leaving now. I'm obliged for the help."

Tolkien looked down at the young man. "Sorry, Mr. Davis, but I'm afraid we can't allow that."

Davis stiffened. He turned to face the Tolkien. "Do you intend to hang me, Mr. Tolkien? To be sure there are no witnesses?"

The old man's voice was low and hard. "You're half right, Mr. Davis."

"We can leave the gray in that fenced pasture—plenty of grass and water—and pick him up later. The captain will understand. But you're coming with us, Mr. Davis. You've got no choice in this matter."

CHAPTER 8

RUNS TOWARD, TOWELS protecting his hands from the heat, carried the heavy blue-enamel roaster from the fire to the table. Sarah, Jimmy, and Rosie—each scrubbed clean and wearing fresh, sun-scented clothing—waited expectantly.

Sarah fidgeted in her chair, staring at the plate and silverware before her, casting furtive glances at her children and this stranger.

Black-eyed Susans and prairie sunflowers leaned from a glass of water set in the center of the table, a splash of color against the weathered gray wood.

Runs Toward set the roaster on the table and opened it. Inside was the loin roast from an antelope, browned in the heat of smoldering buffalo chips. Across the top of the meat were wild onions, lending both flavor and tenderness to the meat.

"Jimmy and I will have to go hunting again tomorrow," Runs Toward said. "But I thought we could have this roast. There's no way to keep the meat in this heat."

The young Cree picked up a butcher knife from the table and began slicing the roast, loading Jimmy's and Rosie's plates with generous helpings. When he tried to serve Sarah, she shook her head.

"Just a little," Runs Toward said, slipping a think slice of meat on her plate. He put the roaster lid on the pan and stepped around the table to take his chair.

"Since I am a guest and you are the man of the house, Jimmy, you should say grace."

Jimmy shook his head.

Runs Toward's voice softened. "Mrs. Wilders, how about you? Would you say grace?"

Sarah Wilders seemed terrified. She tried to push her chair back from the table, but the legs wouldn't slide on the sandstone rock and the chair tipped, almost spilling her over backward.

"C'mon, Mommy. I'm hungry."

Sarah looked at her daughter and smiled, a tentative, sad smile. Her words came slow and halting: "Thank . . . you . . . Lord . . . for the blessings you have bestowed upon us."

"You did real good, Mommy."

"Really well, Rosie. You should have said 'really well,' " Sarah said, surprising herself. The old habit of correcting her children's English was alive still.

"Can we eat now?" Rosie asked.

A nervous smile flickered across Sarah Wilders's face, and the two children attacked the roast. They seemed to race to see which of them could eat the larger share. Sarah picked up her knife and fork and sliced a tiny bit of meat. She tasted the roast tentatively, chewing carefully. "It's good, very good, Mr. . . . ."

"Runs Toward. My name is Runs Toward."

"It's very good, Mr. Runs Toward."

Her children's appetites seemed to cheer Sarah Wilders. She ate a bit more of the roast and tried one of the wild onions.

The sharp taste of the onion, the nourishment of the meat pulled her a little at a time toward full consciousness. She felt the grass tickling her ankles above her button-top shoes. She noticed the acrid scent of cottonwood leaves. Her senses were awakening, and her mind, too. She was trying to bring her life into focus, trying to remember why she seemed now to be emerging from a long, dreamless sleep.

"Jars," she said.

"Jars?" Runs Toward asked.

Sarah pulled herself back in her chair, jamming her fists against her mouth, her elbows to her chest. She hadn't meant to speak. She was simply talking to herself, a habit from the dark days when she believed that she was totally alone, an insignificant speck in the immensity of the Montana prairie. Her eyes darted toward the dugout, and for a moment she longed to be there. But with that longing was a growing awareness that the safety of the dugout was a trap. She didn't want to step into that trap, not ever again.

The words seemed to stick in her throat, and panic spread upward from her throat, pulling her mouth into a thin, straight line, knotting her forehead. She couldn't speak. She was too terrified to speak.

Runs Toward spoke again, the words soft, soothing her fears with the sound of his voice. "You were saying something about jars, Mrs. Wilders?"

Sarah's head tilted to one side, and she shook it in nervous little jerks.

"Were you thinking about canning meat, Mrs. Wilders?"

Sara shook her head and then nodded. "Yes. Canning." Her brow knitted again. "We had jars. . . . I can't remember."

Again the silence. Again the breach in her thought. Again the desperation, and then Rosie spoke.

"We traded them, remember, Mommy? At that town, we traded them for flour."

"Oh, yes, I remember. The lady in the store was so kind. She gave us an extra measure of flour and a little sugar, too."

"I remember," Jimmy said. "You made rolls the next morning. Cinnamon rolls. We were camped beside a little creek, and I had gone fishing. I'll bet I smelled those cinnamon rolls a mile out. I caught some nice catfish, but I couldn't pay any attention to what I was doing, so I came in. Those were the best cinnamon rolls I ever ate."

"Can we have some cinnamon rolls now, Mommy?"

Sarah Wilders looked at her daughter and smiled, and then her face twisted into a frown. "I don't have any flour, or yeast, or sugar. I don't have anything left to make cinnamon rolls. It's all gone. All gone."

Sarah's hands fluttered over the rough top of the table. "This isn't our table. What happened to our table? Jimmy, what happened to our table?"

"We traded it, Ma. Don't you remember? We traded it for repair work on the wagon. That wheelwright in that town . . . I don't remember what town it was."

Sarah's words came flat: "That was my grandmother's table. Walnut. Rubbed with oil until you could see your face in it. I thought that when we had our ranch in Montana I would have a room for that table. I had a matching set of plates and some silver that my grandmother . . ."

She stopped, frowning, as she looked at Jimmy.

He fidgeted in his chair and stared at the meat on his plate. "I don't remember, Ma. I don't remember who got your grandma's silverware."

Sarah leaned back in her chair, her eyes reaching into the light and shadow of the leaves on the cottonwood tree, but she wasn't seeing the leaves. She was watching the miles roll past the wagon's wheels, watching her family moving from one life to the next.

Sarah Wilders glanced across the table at Runs Toward. She felt compelled to tell him how the Wilders family came to this isolation on the Montana prairie, without jars to can meat, without her grandmother's table.

But she didn't know how to begin, where to start. Her mind flitted from thought to thought, landing only long enough to discard one approach and go searching for another.

She sighed and then smiled sadly at Rosie. "Rosie, would you get your pretties to show Mr. Runs Toward?"

Rosie beamed. She skipped over to the dugout, disappearing into its blackness, and Runs Toward thought he saw Sarah shudder as her daughter disappeared into that dark shadow. The girl returned a moment later with a cigar box. She carried it in both hands, as though it contained the Queen of England's crown jewels. She placed the box on the table and opened the lid carefully, almost reverently.

"See?" she said, taking a blue feather from the box. "I found this at home. Isn't it pretty? It's a feather from a bluebird. Someday, I want to have a dress this color. Mommy said I could . . . someday."

Rosie reached again into the box. "Here's a card from Aunt Agnes. She sent it to me from St. Louis, Misery."

"Missouri," Sarah corrected gently. "Your grandpa just called it Misery."

"Oh," the little girl said, dipping into the box again. "This is the picture I drew of Jesus in Sunday school. Have you ever seen Jesus, Mr. Runs?"

"Yes, I believe I have," Runs Toward said softly.

"Oh, and this!" Rosie reached once more into the box, gently retrieving a rose, long since dried and shriveled. "This was the rose I put on Grandma's cack . . . ?"

"Casket, Rosie. You put that on Grandma's casket."

"But I took it back."

Sarah Wilders nodded and smiled.

Rosie looked beaming at Runs Toward. "Aren't my pretties something?" she asked.

"Yes," Runs Toward whispered.

The little girl's excitement seemed to charge her mother with energy. When first she began to speak, her words were flat, emotionless, as though she were reading from a dull book. But as she spoke, the words took on a life of their own. They seemed to energize Sarah Wilders, bringing a gentle flush of color to her cheeks and life to her eyes.

Runs Toward sat in his chair, enthralled.

"We sifted through all the things that our lives had been," Sarah Wilders said. "We picked each of the things that we would need when we found our ranch in Montana. We took harness and rope and cooking gear and nails and saws and hammers. We brought rifles and the brand Samuel had the blacksmith make right after we were married. A four-leaf clover: 'For luck,' he always said. For the luck we would need.

"And when we had all the things we could think of that we would need, we picked our treasures, just like Rosie did. We picked the things that reminded us who we were. Grandma's table and the old mantel clock and the silverware. It seemed to me then that our whole lives were in the wagon—what we had been, what we were, and what we would be.

"It was cold, at first, early spring with spitting rain and some snow and blustery days. We put Friend, Nebraska, behind us with all the people we knew there, the church, the school, the general store . . ."

Rosie jumped into the reminiscing. "With the licorice candy. The store had the best licorice candy ever."

Sarah looked at her daughter and smiled. "Yes, the best licorice candy ever."

"From the moment we left, I felt as though we were on a ship. . . . I've never been on a ship before. Have you, Mr. Runs Toward?"

He shook his head.

"I suppose it was the grass. It waves at the wind in its passing. It ripples as though God had just cast a huge stone on the prairie.

"It seemed that we were on a ship that had lost its anchor and was adrift, carried by the vagaries of the current. We moved so slowly that sometimes it seemed we were standing still and the world was edging past, curious to see this family that marched so solemnly in place.

"But we didn't just drift along. The current was full of snags and sandbars and shallow water. We didn't ever see these things coming until we were upon them, but it wouldn't have made any difference, anyway, because we had no way to steer the ship.

"The treasures went first. We traded the things that we didn't *need*. We didn't *need* the table and the clock and the silverware. Samuel told me that, and I knew he was right. We could run a ranch without my grandmother's silverware.

"But each time, I felt I was losing a piece of what I was, losing some of the anchors that held me in place against that current. They tied me to my grandmother and grandfather, to what I had been and what I was. They were my treasure box, Mr. Runs Toward. . . .

"And then we began losing the things that we needed. We had a small herd at the beginning, just breeding stock. Oh, you should have seen Samuel driving that stock. Being on a horse behind a herd—even a herd as small as ours— that was his first love. He would come in at night after bedding the cattle and horses, all excited about planning the next day."

Sarah's voice drifted off into silence, her eyes clouding as she stared blindly at the prairie's distant horizon.

Runs Toward waited until he could feel the silence as he could feel the heat, and then he spoke. "Mrs. Wilders?"

She looked at him, and for a moment he fell into her eyes and came up gasping.

"Mrs. Wilders?" The words squeaked through his constricted throat.

Her eyes cleared, and she continued.

"And the distance . . ." Sarah Wilders shook her head in wonder. "We had cut ourselves adrift with no destination, just a vague idea. We were carried along by the prairie winds bound for whatever foreign shore, and then Jolly broke his leg."

Sarah's eyes fluttered across the table and then reached up to stare at the young Cree. "He was a fine horse. Never balked. Pulled long after we ran out of oats. Oh, Samuel took fine care of him. Evenings he would curry the horses, hobble them along the streams when he could so they would have the best, the greenest grasses to eat . . ."

Sarah's voice softened until it was almost breathless. "Sometimes I wished that he would spend as much time with me as he did with the horses, but . . ."

She realized what she had said then, and her hands fluttered up to her temples and she brushed her hair, damp still from its washing, behind her ears.

"I don't mean to criticize. I mean . . ."

"I know," Runs Toward said. "Go on."

"Well, I saw the tree. It had been so long since we had seen a tree. I was thinking how nice it would be to sit on cool grass in the shade of a tree, to listen to the wind rustle the leaves. So we came here, walking behind the wagon so the burden wouldn't be too great for Jack.

"It seemed to me that the prairie winds were washing us ashore, then. As though this was the place they had meant us to be. The tree seemed to be—I don't know—magic."

She looked at Runs Toward out of the corner of her eyes. "That sounds crazy, doesn't it?"

He shook his head.

"And you, Mr. Runs Toward? How did you happen to come here?"

"I had a dream," he murmured. "About this tree."

He stopped, looking into the tree's lower limbs, trying to remember that scene from his dream. "I think this tree is magic, too, Mrs. Wilders. I tried to run from it, but I couldn't resist its pull and now I'm here. I don't think I can leave . . . unless you and your children leave, Mrs. Wilders.

"Your wagon is drying out; the winds are sucking the

moisture from the wood. It won't be long before the rims fall off its wheels, before dust clogs its hubs.

"I have two horses, Mrs. Wilders. I can take you and your children to safety. It's not so far to Fort Benton. We can find help for you there. You could wait there for your husband."

Fear crossed Sarah's face.

"No, Mr. Runs Toward. We have nothing left to trade, nothing more to give up. If we left here, Samuel wouldn't know where we were. He would think that we left him alone on the prairie, that we deserted him.

"It is terrible to be abandoned on the prairie, Mr. Runs Toward. I wouldn't want him to think that we had deserted out in the midst of all . . . this." Her hand, pale from her sojourn in the dugout, swept across the horizon. She jerked it back into her lap, as though afraid that the prairie might snatch it, take it away, too.

"Mrs. Wilders, I'm sure your husband would have come back if he could. He might have been injured or—"

"No, no, no, no, no," Sarah was shaking her head. "No, nothing has happened to him. He'll be back, Mr. Runs Toward. He'll be back. He wouldn't leave us alone, not out here. He wouldn't do that."

Runs Toward whispered, "We could tack a note up on the tree. Tell him where we've gone."

Sarah Wilders's eyes were open wide, pupils larger than they should be on a day still bright with the summer sun.

"The wind would take it away," she said. "Out here the wind takes everything away."

Jick-Jack Snyder, who would pause in the midst of a stampede to play a game of pitch, had been sidling up to Ryder Davis since the shooting.

Eli Gilfeather saw no glory in the killing of Jean LaFontaine, and he was sure Ryder Davis did not either. Gilfeather had read more sorrow than triumph in Davis's face when he knelt to cross LaFontaine's hands and close his eyes.

The shooting nagged at Gilfeather. It lacked anger, the heat of the moment; it seemed more like the mercy killing of a horse with a broken leg than the murder of a man.

LaFontaine was an outlaw of the first order, a stealer of horses and probably a killer of men. When he stood before his accusers that morning, he was cool as a November morning.

But Ryder Davis had LaFontaine beaten for pure gall. He faced that double-barreled shotgun without a flicker of fear. When LaFontaine jerked the muzzle toward Davis, the cowboy reached for his pistol as casually as he might swat a fly.

Gilfeather remembered again the sound of the bullet striking flesh, the round hole that appeared in the breed's forehead. That was one hell of a shot for a man in a hurry, but Davis hadn't seemed to be in a hurry. The movement was fluid, natural. Davis seemed nothing so much as an experienced workman doing a job that needed doing.

Gilfeather sat on a long-dead juniper stump, feeling the heat of the fire on his legs while the chill of a Montana night played with his back. He shuddered, not sure whether the tremor that ran across his shoulders came from the cold or from the scene that kept playing across his mind.

He stared across the fire at the knot of men surrounding Ryder Davis. Jick-Jack was beginning to strut, courting Davis's attention.

Eli shook his head, staring into the fire.

"Hell, it's natural," Tolkien said.

"What's natural?"

"The ritual," Tolkien said. "You've been watching the men cozy up to Mr. Davis. Nothing new in that. Probably been that way forever."

"What in the hell are you talking about?"

"You're wondering why Jick-Jack is throwing himself at Mr. Davis," the old man continued. "That's the way of it. Weak men always cozy up to the powerful. Right now, Mr. Davis is bull goose."

The old man picked up a branch and stirred the embers of the fire. "You see, a woman can give life, and that makes that gender about the most powerful set of creatures on this earth. A man can't give life—he can set the ember a-glowing, but he can't blow it into flame. About the most powerful thing a man can do is take life.

"Mr. Davis took a life this morning, so that makes him bull goose in the camp, at least for tonight. Come tomorrow morning, I'll be bull goose again.

"Tonight, every one of those yahoos over there is trying to touch that source of power, to revitalize their miserable lives. Every one of them is wondering what it was like to face that man with a double-barreled shotgun and shoot him to death, clean as you please.

"Some of them—like Jick-Jack there—they want to have that same power. Power is what life is about, Mr. Gilfeather. Nothing more, nothing less. Jick-Jack, he's feeling the heat of that power same as you and I are feeling the heat from the fire. He's going to want more of that feeling, Mr. Gilfeather. He's going to want it so bad that he'll be willing to kill for it."

The old man picked up the stick and stirred the fire again. "A little bit of the killer lives in all of us. Just like these coals, all it takes is a puff of wind at the right, or wrong, time to fan the flame.

"The killing will get easier as we go through this. Some will take a liking to it. Jick-Jack will be like that. He'll take to killing because that's the only power that pathetic son of a bitch will ever know."

Gilfeather whispered, "What about you, Mr. Tolkien? If he does your killing for you, is that what makes you bull goose?"

Tolkien chuckled. "You're a fool, Mr. Gilfeather, but you aren't as stupid as I thought you were."

Davis left the little knot of admirers and poured himself a cup of coffee, settling beside the fire to stare into the flames. His eyes, light blue in the sunshine, glowed white in the fire's light. He looked across the flames at Tolkien.

"What did you mean when you said I couldn't leave and I asked if you were going to hang me so I wouldn't talk?"

Gilfeather glanced at Tolkien. Davis's implicit challenge was not lost on the old man. He grinned wolfishly.

"You know damn well what we're doing out here. Hell, the papers have been full of it. They've been chattering for months about how if the territory won't control the rustlers, then the sheriffs should call a posse to handle the trouble."

"Well, the sheriffs didn't, so—"

"So the Cattlemen's Association formed a committee of vigilantes."

"Told you that you knew damn well what we're doing out here." The old man grinned again. "Each of these men is sworn to secrecy, but that doesn't mean spit. I know they're not going to talk about what's going on out here because the same lawmen who won't do a damn thing about rustlers would likely hang any vigilantes they found. None of these men will talk . . . but you aren't a vigilante, and I can't let you go."

Davis's face stiffened just a little, and for a moment Gilfeather would have sworn that his eyes picked up a shine from the fire the way the eyes of animals do. Davis and Tolkien were two prairie wolves staring at each other across the fire, each ready to go for the other's throat.

"You got that half right," Davis said, the words little more than a whisper.

A grin crossed Tolkien's face, but it died as fast as the sparks that swirled up from the campfire died in the black night air.

"Can't leave witnesses," Tolkien said.

"I'm no witness. I shot him. LaFontaine probably had a lot of friends. I don't want it out that I tripped the hammer on him."

"Self-defense," the old man said. "He was aiming to blow two holes through you. No jury would convict you of killing him."

"His friends might."

"Maybe. Maybe not. They're not going to hear about it from these boys. Seems to me there wouldn't be much risk to you to speak your piece to the local sheriff."

Davis leaned toward the fire, flames playing across his face, leaving his eyes and cheeks in dark shadows. "I told you before, I'm no damn vigilante."

The old man stirred the fire, and a column of sparks rose in the dark air. He stared through the sparks at Davis.

Eli shuddered. He was looking at the face of Satan warming himself at the fires of hell. When the old man spoke, his voice rumbling from deep in his throat, he seemed more than ever to be the fallen angel.

"You're going to ride with us until you get your hands dirty," Tolkien said. "When they're dirty enough that you can't wash them clean, then you'll be free to go. Then, and not one moment before then, Mr. Davis."

CHAPTER 9

... Billy Blue whirled and shot Snaky Pete in the gut, knowing that the outlaw would be a long time dying. Billy Blue didn't like back shooters, especially when they were trying to shoot him in the back.

He stopped then, dropping his empty shells in the street and reloading his Colt .44. In the Far West, a cowboy had to be ready for all eventualities. ...

SIMON HARDIN CLOSED the book with a sigh. He was a thoughtful young man in love with words. He longed to be a writer, and he had studied the classics, searching between the lines for the subtleties and nuances that tell the real stories. He had picked up his first dime novel of the true West as a lark but it had taken no time for him to become enthralled.

First there was the land, rugged, unsettled, and boundless. The land put men and women in perspective, left them soft-spoken and steel-spined. They "doctored" snake bites by soaking the wounded appendage in a bucket of coal oil or resorted to some other home remedy, and when someone broke the rigid code that ruled the land, they "doctored" that, too.

Courts and sheriffs and the government in Washington were more concepts than realities on these western plains. Keen-eyed men rendered justice with .44 Colts hanging like Excalibur from their hips. These were men who respected men with honor and despised those without it. These were men who placed their women on pedestals worthy of Maid Marian.

This was a land as large as Simon Hardin's imagination. The young man turned to stare out the window of the jolting train car. The train was speeding, at an incredible twenty-five to thirty-five miles per hour, across country controlled no more than eight years ago by the Sioux and Cheyenne, the Crow and Arapaho. He wondered if he would see any of these fierce warriors racing across the prairie on their war ponies to stare through the train windows at their white adversaries.

The country was immense. He had left his home near the Boston Harbor to come west, to write about this exciting new world with clarity and perception so fresh his readers would marvel.

Simon looked out the window at the Yellowstone River winding beneath the cottonwood trees in the afternoon sun. Soon Simon would be in the new town of Billings, and then he would head north to Uncle Obadiah's.

Simon reached into the vest pocket of his jacket, pulled out the letter. His eyes went over the words, his mind hearing them spoken in Uncle Obadiah's rich baritone.

Dear Simon,

I take great pleasure in the anticipation I feel of seeing you once again. Separated as I am from my family by these thousands of miles, I would much appreciate your visit.

I must say that your decision to attempt "cowboying," as you put it, raises certain apprehensions in my mind. This is hard, dangerous work. One never knows when one of these range horses, usually green broke, will spook at a change of the wind and dump you unceremoniously on the prairie.

But if you intend to attempt this life and your father has no objections, I can only help to make it as positive an experience for you as possible. I have always been fond of you, and since my marriage is without issue and I without heir, perhaps you will choose to stay on.

Please pass my regards to your father, mother, and siblings. I miss them all and intend to travel east this next winter to reacquaint myself with the more gentle life there.

With great affection, I await your arrival. I shall have a

man at Fort Maginnis July first to await your arrival with one of the teamsters. If you should not arrive that day, I will send him the next week, on the eighth day of July.

> Sincerely,
> Obadiah S. Hardin
> In the year of our Lord
> 1884

Simon folded the letter and put it away. Already the West had put its print on his uncle. "Green broke" and "spook" would have tangled his tongue just a few years ago in Boston, but now they rolled easily off his pen. Simon was looking forward to seeing his uncle and meeting his uncle's wife, the Cree "princess" Obadiah described in his letters.

Now he leaned back in his chair, watching the landscape flee past. The rail track swung just a little away from the river at this point, trapping a band of antelope between train and water. They raced the train, passing it easily and crossing the track ahead of the engine.

Simon Hardin's mind was racing, too—running ahead as the antelope had, running ahead toward his great adventure.

The Northern Pacific engine and train rattled across the east bridge over the Yellowstone River and into Billings. The town had the stamp of the railroad on it. Frederick Billings, president of the Northern Pacific until its takeover by the Oregon Railway and Navigation Company, had chosen this city to be his namesake.

Simon could see why. The town nestled in a tree-covered river valley between spectacular rimrocks. Already the streets bustled with men of enterprise, women dressed in the height of eastern fashion.

But the West—the real West that Simon had come to find—was in evidence, too. Rough men in rough clothes and wide-brimmed hats leaned against the door of a saloon across the street. Scattered here and there in the shade of city buildings were blanket-draped reminders of the once mighty plain tribes.

The scene captivated Simon Hardin. He collected his baggage and dropped it in front of a bench at the depot, rummaging through one bag for a pencil and the diary he kept there. He sat straight and stiff on the bench, too excited to lean back, eyes darting from the scene in front of him to the words flowing on the pages of the diary propped on his knee.

Simon Hardin was sketching Billings with words. He was making a record of what he saw and felt on this first day in the Montana Territory, on this first day in the real West. One night in a hotel, and then he would travel north in a wagon bearing supplies for Fort Maginnis. Uncle Obadiah had sent men to meet him there.

Crack! The bullwhip uncurled and snapped beside the onside mare's ear. She shook her head and danced to the side.

"That'll teach you, Mary Belle."

The teamster Moby Wilmot leaned over the side of the freight wagon to spit a stream of tobacco juice at a horned toad sitting beside the road. The toad canted its head and opened one eye as though offended by the old man's manners.

Simon Hardin, eager to capture the essence of life on the plains, asked, "Why did you do that?"

The teamster canted his head and raised one eyebrow, "What? Spit?"

"No, why did you pop the whip at that horse?"

"Mary Belle?"

"Yes."

"She's been raising her tail to me."

They rode a while then in silence—as much silence, at

any rate, as there can be on a squeaking, jolting freight wagon tied to eight horses with a jangling harness.

Simon broke the silence.

"What do you mean, she's been raising her tail to you?"

"Fartin'."

"Isn't that natural for a horse?"

"Don't mind a horse doin' it once in a while. You know what they say?"

Simon shook his head, and the teamster shook his in disgust. "You greenhorns are all alike."

"Is that what *they* say?"

"Moby Wilmot leaned the top half of his five-foot, six-inch frame forward to stare back into Simon's eyes.

"*They* say that a fartin' horse never tires and a fartin' man is the man to hire."

"Then why did you pop the whip at . . . Mary Belle?"

The teamster shook his head again. "Bad enough to be ridin' along with a chatterbox without havin' a horse raisin' her tail to you, too. Hell, go into a bar after a trip with a tail-raisin' horse and everybody sidles away from you."

Discretion kept Simon from saying that it wasn't a tail-raising horse that made people shy away from the teamster. It was obvious to anyone within ten feet of Moby Wilmot that he didn't waste any time soaking in a tub.

Silence reigned for the next quarter mile.

"Well, hell," Moby said. "I don't suppose you'll stop nagging me until I tell you. Mary Belle is upset because I combed Old Blue out before her.

"Always curry Mary Belle first, but I spotted this tick on Old Blue. All swole up with blood, it was. Big as a dime. So I pulled it off, and as long as I was there, I curried Old Blue first. Didn't mean anything by it, but Mary Belle has been raising her tail to me ever since." Wilmot glowered. "Some trip this has been. Got a chatterbox for a passenger and old Mary Belle is raising her tail to me. Whoo-ee, I can't even smell the sagebrush anymore. I think my nose is all wore out."

"Mr. Wilmot, I said, 'Good morning' on the first day of this trek. I won't ever do that again. Today, I asked one simple question. I don't see how that makes me a chatterbox."

"Well, *la-de-da*," Wilmot said.

Silence stretched for another half mile.

Moby Wilmot turned on the wagon seat to stare at Simon through squinted eyes. "You want to climb down off this wagon seat and have a go at me, greenhorn?"

Simon was perplexed. "Why would I want to fight you?"

"If you didn't want to fight, why the hell did you call me a liar?"

"I didn't call you a liar."

"Did, too."

"How?"

"I said you were a chatterbox. You said you weren't. Pretty plain to me you called me a liar."

Simon sighed. "Mr. Wilmot, it was not my intention to call you a liar. I apologize."

"Well, you got some sense, anyway."

"Thank you."

"I said some sense. I didn't say you were a damn genius nor nothing like that. Enough sense, anyway, to see that I'd make short work of you."

"I can see that all right," Simon said, shaking his head.

"You mockin' me?"

"Mocking you?"

"You heard me."

"No, Mr. Wilmot, I am not mocking you."

"Good thing for you."

"Yes," Simon said. "That's a good thing for me."

Silence stretched for nearly another mile, and then Moby Wilmot pulled his horses to a stop and set his hand brake.

Simon Hardin looked at the teamster in frustration. "What? Do we have to fight, now?"

"You're really on the prod, ain't you, greenhorn? Well, you climb down off that seat, and we'll settle this once and for all."

"Mr. Wilmot"—Simon's words came out with a sigh—"if I have offended you in any way, I apologize. I certainly had no intention of doing that. Please forgive me."

"Well, hell," Wilmot said. "As long as you say you're sorry."

The two sat silent on the wagon seat for five minutes, five long minutes, and then Wilmot spoke again. "Well, damn it all to hell! Climb down! Can't you understand plain English!"

Simon Hardin gritted his teeth and jumped from the wagon, landing with a thump on the Montana prairie.

"You win, Mr. Wilmot. I'm down. Now, let's finish this, here and now."

Silence stretched again and Simon's anger fled, leaving him standing limp.

Wilmot shook his head in disgust. "You are the feistiest greenhorn I ever did see. Don't know why you're on the prod so. If I was you, I would just take my fancy new saddle and take to walking."

Simon's eyes blinked shut and he rubbed his fingers across his forehead as though to rub out a sudden headache. When he spoke, his words came in a whisper.

"Mr. Wilmot, I don't understand what you want me to do."

Wilmot's eyes rolled in disgust. "I take it back," the teamster said.

"Take *what* back?"

"What I said about you not being stupid. You're every bit as stupid as any greenhorn I ever saw."

Both of Simon's hands went to his temples, gently massaging away the pain. "Thank you, Mr. Wilmot. I appreciate your kind words. Now, will you tell me where I am supposed to go with my 'fancy new saddle'?"

Wilmot shook his head. "I declare," he whispered, seeking in Mary Belle's rump the answer to this perplexing problem. "Try to follow me now, son. Now, you was to have been at Fort Maginnis on July first. Right?" The teamster turned to stare at Simon.

Simon nodded.

"Now, this is July fourth. You with me so far?"

Simon nodded.

"So, you're not at Fort Maginnis on July first. You getting my drift, boy?"

"I'm with you so far," Simon said, squeezing his skull between his palms.

"So, your uncle won't have a man at Fort Maginnis when you get there. You'll be stuck there four more days. Now, you don't want to be stuck there, do you?"

Simon shook his head.

"So, if you get off here, you can follow this crick to your left all the way up to your uncle's place. You can be there in a couple of days, even carrying that fancy new saddle. I'll give you some jerky." The teamster's eyes narrowed into a glare. "Ah, hell, I'll give you a can of peaches, too, although I was aiming to give them to Mary Belle to see if I could talk her into not raising her tail to me." Moby Wilmot shook his head and rolled his eyes, repugnance showing on his face. "I'll smell to high heaven thanks to you, greenhorn."

Simon's teeth gritted shut. "Thank you, Mr. Wilmot, but I don't think I can take all the credit."

"Well, that's all right." Wilmot crooked his neck and continued in a more conciliatory manner. "You just follow the crick north. Find a nice place to spend the night and you'll be all right. Don't step on any rattlesnakes and they'll leave you alone. Not much else out here that will bother you."

The teamster fidgeted in his seat. "Son, what the hell do I have to say to you to get you to take your damn saddle?"

Simon tugged down his saddle, and Wilmot dug through a burlap sack at his feet for some jerky and a can of peaches.

"That'll be four bits," Wilmot said, "for haulin' the saddle. The jerky and the can of peaches is free."

Simon handed the teamster a fifty-cent piece. "Thank you."

"Ah, hell, you ain't so bad for a greenhorn chatterbox. Say hello to your uncle for me."

Simon nodded. He climbed the hill behind him, taking a seat on a sandstone ledge protruding from the lip of the hill. Below, Moby Wilmot slapped his reins on his horses and the wagon continued north and a little west toward the fort.

Simon watched the wagon leave, followed by a plume of dust. About two hundred yards ahead, the trail took a sharp curve to the right. Just before the team disappeared around the corner, Mary Belle lifted her tail.

Wilmot's voice came like a rumble of thumber, lightning intruding occasionally with particularly pungent phrases about Mary Belle's lineage and her probable fate once the teamster reached Fort Maginnis. Then, the wagon disappeared around the corner, only a soft plume of dust and the crack of Moby Wilmot's whip offering evidence that it ever existed.

The rumble began low in Simon Jacob's throat, swelling until a full-fledged guffaw rolled across the prairie, sending a flock of sage hen lumbering into the air from the deep grass and brush beside the creek.

He slipped the jerky and the can of peaches into his saddlebags, vowing to keep the peaches for a special occasion or to treat an especially flatulent horse.

Already, Simon Hardin loved Montana. He stood, shouldering his saddle and walking north toward his uncle's ranch and his new life, his feet marching to the call of the July sun, in rhythm with a meadowlark's call.

CHAPTER 10

JICK-JACK SNYDER SLOUCHED hip and shoulder against the trunk of a cottonwood tree, chewing a stalk of bunchgrass.

The other vigilantes gathered around Ryder Davis, chuckling occasionally and passing glances at each other as they listened to some story spoken too softly for Eli Gilfeather to hear.

"Interesting, isn't it?" Old Man Tolkien was bemused, as though he were watching a spider build a web. "Mr. Snyder has taken the second step."

"What the hell are you talking about?"

"People, Mr. Gilfeather. People. Some men travel all over the globe looking for exotic animals and plants. Others search the heavens to find the root of creation. But people are the most fascinating of all subjects."

"Well, I'm pretty damn fascinated, Your Highness, but if it's all the same to you, I'll pass. I need some sleep."

"It isn't all the same to me, Mr. Gilfeather. I realize that you don't understand half of what I tell you, but that's part of your charm. I can speak to you as I spoke to one of my family's hounds when I was a child. If only I could train you to look at me with the same adoring eyes he did."

Tolkien's grin was evil, pure evil. The old man continued, "The point, Mr. Gilfeather, is power. The point is always power. You have no power over me. No matter how outrageously I speak to you, you can manage little more than a roll of the eyes to contradict me. I own you, Mr. Gilfeather."

Gilfeather's words came without rancor. "You don't own me any more than I own that fire. As long as I keep feeding it, the fire provides me with a little warmth and light, but no one owns it."

"Following your analogy, Mr. Gilfeather, you must realize that the fire exists only so long as you want it to. If you stop feeding it, nothing but a patch of cold black ashes would remain. That's the way it is with us. Your existence depends upon me. That is power, Mr. Gilfeather. That is absolute power."

Tolkien threw another stick on the fire, as though to drive home his point. Then he said, "I was speaking about Mr. Jick-Jack Snyder. He has taken the second step in his quest for power. He had been basking in Mr. Davis's glory after the shooting, but now he believes himself to be empowered. He looks at the other men gathered around Mr. Davis as sycophants, while he is part of the royal circle.

"The next step for Mr. Snyder will be the exercise of the power that he now feels. Watch, Mr. Gilfeather. Sometime in the next few days, Mr. Snyder will do something to exercise his newfound power in front of the other men. Mark my words."

"You're as full of crap as a Christmas goose."

Tolkien's shoulders shook; for a moment, Gilfeather thought the old man was choking. But the shudders came from laughter, the most derisive laughter Gilfeather had ever witnessed.

"I'll tell you something, old man," Gilfeather said ominously. "You might think you own me, but you decide to put out my fire, you better be damn sure you get it completely out. One ember that looks cold and dead as hell can start a wildfire. And you're going to be downwind from that fire, old man. No matter which way the wind is blowing, you're going to be downwind."

Gilfeather rose and stalked to his bedroll. Old Man Tolkien's eyes followed. He wasn't smiling now. He poured the remainder of the pot of coffee on the fire and crushed the coals beneath the soles of his boots.

*   *   *

Jick-Jack Snyder slipped from his bedroll into pure darkness. He had been awake when Tolkien toured the sleeping men, stirring them into activity.

"Moving out now . . . Want to circle Fort Maginnis . . . Don't want to be spotted by any patrols . . . Only a matter of time until they find the breed . . . Want to be shut of this country before then . . . No fire—no coffee."

Jick-Jack had stayed up late the night before, riding too many cups of coffee and a sense of excitement he didn't understand. He had slept only in bits and pieces, his mind returning time after time to the scene at the rustler's cabin. But over the night, the scene changed. In Jick-Jack's mind, he, not Ryder Davis, spurred his horse in front of the tense cowboys. He, not Ryder Davis, whispered with the certainty of death: "I'm telling you that if you make one move with that shotgun, I'll put a bullet right between your eyes."

Jick-Jack saw his hand moving in a blur to the pistol at his side, thumbing back the hammer as the muzzle swung up to settle on LaFontaine's forehead. His finger teased the trigger, and Jick-Jack sent a hardcase rustler with a double-barreled scattergun to his death.

Jick-Jack saw himself on a dancing horse in front of the other cowboys, watching the respect and fear grow in their eyes as they saw him revealed for the first time in his true colors, a cool, seasoned fighter who could snuff a man's life out with the casualness of a cook swatting a fly.

Jick-Jack's neck swelled with the thoughts, the way a mule deer buck's neck swells in the fall rutting season. The cowboy strutted a little with that thought as he stepped onto the prairie, darkest just before the dawn. He stopped to relieve himself, listening for the shuffling feet of hobbled horses.

The air was cool and black and sweet.

*   *   *

The men rode in darkness, following a creek bottom even blacker than the prairie around them. The creek led them nearly due south away from Fort Maginnis, away from La-Fontaine, dead with a bullet to the brain and hanging from the peak of his cabin's roof.

In death, Jean LaFontaine rode with the men now. He had followed them to their bedrolls the night before, and he was with them in the morning when they awakened. They looked into the darkness and saw his face, twisted and distorted by the bullet hole in his forehead, by the rope around his neck.

The vigilantes tried to steer their thoughts away from LaFontaine to happy times in their favorite saloons with their favorite women. They tried to concentrate on past adventures, like the time when that wolf wandered into camp and sat down at the fire like he belonged there . . . Or how Ginger Gramus, meanest man alive, rode into that stampede to save the cook he hated and they both went down.

Always those thoughts flickered and disappeared, leaving the men to ponder LaFontaine's death.

Night began to give way to dawn, as light came tiptoeing into the world. Just as the sun cracked the horizon, at that single moment when morning is sweetest, they saw him lying flat on the prairie, still as death.

Old Man Tolkien raised his hand then and they stopped, jockeying their horses silently into position so they could evaluate this anomaly. They knew that the dark shape reclining on the prairie was a man. The silhouette was outlined sharply in the morning light. Their eyes, ears, and noses tested the scene for clues. Death came easy on the prairie, and that was their first thought, but the man's head rested against a saddle. Dead men didn't usually slip into eternity that comfortably. There was no scent of death on the prairie, and no scavengers or vultures had come to feast.

The men studied the shadows for morning light glinting from blued rifle barrels, but surely no ambush would be set so carelessly as this.

Tolkien dropped his hand, and the men edged forward, as silent as possible astride horses whose saddles creaked and whose bridles jangled. The men rode in a semicircle at the feet of the man on the prairie.

The stranger was a youth, little more than a boy. The redness of his face was testimony to his lack of time in the prairie sun. His suit, vest, and coat, carefully folded on a blanket, were well made and foreign to the Montana prairie. He slept very soundly, his head resting on a fancy saddle that had not yet felt the rub of a man's britches or the sweat from a horse's back.

"Rustler," Jick-Jack whispered.

One of the cowboys from the Circle Jay glared at Jick-Jack. "Why in the hell do you think he's a rustler?"

"Why else would he have a saddle and no horse?"

"Horse might have broken his leg."

"That saddle ain't even been used. This slick came out here to rustle himself a horse."

"Jick-Jack, you're getting soft in the head."

It was Jick-Jack's turn to glare. His voice rumbled up from his belly, "Watch what you say, four-flusher."

"Listen, you silly son of a bitch. Don't you call me a four-flusher."

"You ain't never paid me that ninety-six cents you owed me from last year's roundup."

"Don't owe you, saw you take that ace from the bottom of the deck, plain as your face."

"You son of a bitch!" The words came loud and menacing. The words woke Simon Hardin.

The young man's eyes blinked open. He was looking into a sky still gray from the night; he was surrounded by men on horseback, men with three days of beard grizzling their faces. Men dressed in wool pants and shirts, wide-brimmed hats set at jaunty angles on their heads. They had a wildness to them, a hardness, but Hardin could see the immensity of the prairie in their eyes, a quiet confidence in the way they sat their horses.

These were the men Hardin had come to write about. Knights of the plain touched with the scent of horse dung. Tough, hard men with a sense of nobility. His eyes searched each of them, looking for details, seeking clues to their lives from the way they dressed, from the ropes and rifles hanging from their horses. The old man was their leader. No doubt about that.

They seemed wild, and Jacobs was taken with the thought that he might share with them the can of peaches that the teamster Moby Wilmot had given him. Draw them to him with the promise of a treat, as he might call a skittish horse into a corral.

Jacobs started to roll to one side so he could stand.

"Hold it right there, rustler."

"Rustler?" Hardin stared at Jick-Jack Snyder.

"Just lay still." The speaker, a little man with an air of menace, prodded his horse toward the reclining man. He seemed nervous, almost jerky in his movements.

Simon Hardin realized that the man was out of control, dangerous.

The cowboy said, "I'm telling you that if you make one move with that shotgun, I'll put a bullet right between your eyes."

The words had run through Jick-Jack's mind so many times that they came by rote, without thought. He realized what he had said when some of the vigilantes snickered. The sound stabbed into his ego. The other men weren't supposed to laugh. Jick-Jack was making his play with an outlaw, the same as Ryder Davis had. The others should be watching him with the same fear and respect that they had shown Ryder Davis as he stepped in front of the rustler Jean LaFontaine.

"Shotgun?" Hardin asked, bewildered. "I have no shotgun."

The snickers spread through the cowboys.

"I'm no rustler," Hardin said. "Here, I'll show you." He reached then for the letter his uncle had sent him, the letter that would explain why he was sleeping alone on the prairie.

He didn't see Jick-Jack reaching for his pistol. He didn't see the muzzle swinging for his forehead. He didn't feel the bullet that sprayed his brains on the saddle.

"Got him. Got the son of a bitch just like I said I would: right between the eyes."

Jick-Jack stepped off his horse, running to the body, trying to remember in his excitement what he was supposed to do next. Kneel on the ground. Close the victim's eyes.

No! That was Ryder Davis. Jick-Jack Snyder was claiming this kill as his own.

Jick-Jack knelt beside the body. "Hey, boys. Look at this saddle." He saw then the gray tissue of the brain sticking around a black hole burned in the leather, and when he next spoke, his voice was shaky. "Hell, brains won't hurt it. Injuns use brains to cure the leather. Brains won't hurt it at all. Could be he's got some money on him. He looks like he might have some money. Anyway, I get his pistol. I get that."

The men were chillingly silent. No one else had moved.

Jick-Jack flipped open Simon Hardin's vest. He found no pistol, only a letter worn in the reading.

"No pistol." The words dribbled from Jick-Jack's mouth, and he stood suddenly as though to separate himself from the body.

He turned to face the men around him. In the soft light of dawn they seemed ashen, as though the shooting had burned the life from them. Jick-Jack tried to meet their eyes, but they looked away.

Jick-Jack was alone, more alone than he had ever been.

"I thought he was going for his pistol," Jick-Jack whispered. "I wouldn't have shot him if I didn't think . . . Must be a rustler. What else would he be doing out here?"

The pleas fell dead on the prairie, dead as the young man.

Tolkien's voice rumbled into the scene. "Read the letter, Mr. Snyder."

Jick-Jack looked frantically at the old man, his head shaking his denial. "Can't read."

"I'll read it." Ryder Davis leaped from his horse, stalking to the body. He reached down and pulled the letter from Jacobs's vest.

Davis removed his hat and held it with his left hand across his chest. In his right hand, he held the letter up to the light of the sun rising in the east.

"Letter's from Obadiah S. Hardin," Ryder said, and apprehension rippled across the vigilantes. Hardin was one of the biggest ranchers in the territory, his place not more than a few hours north. Hardin had a reputation for treating his men well and his enemies badly.

Light played across Davis's blond hair, and his eyes seemed almost to glow in the early-morning sun. His voice came softly, clearly in the cool air as he read the letter.

When he finished no one spoke. A magpie cawed in the distance, sunlight glinting off its wings. The bird rowed into the morning air and then glided, bursts of energy and grace intertwined, seeking food, always seeking food.

Jick-Jack stood by the body, life leaking from him as it had from Simon Hardin.

Jick-Jack was trying to convince the men—himself—that he had done nothing wrong.

"How the hell could I know? How could I know who he was? We all thought he was a rustler. Being out here on the prairie with a saddle and no horse—he had to be a rustler."

He looked at the men, desperately seeking the slightest

nods indicating that they agreed with him. No one nodded.

Tolkien spurred his horse to the front of the vigilantes. Jick-Jack Snyder looked up at him. "How the hell was I to know? How was I to know?"

Tolkien looked at Snyder with contempt. "See what else he has, Mr. Snyder."

Snyder, grateful for some directions, dropped to his knees and began pawing through Simon Jacobs's clothing. "Hey, here's some money—"

"Leave it."

"But—"

"Leave it!"

Snyder winced and went back to his search.

"A can of peaches."

"Bring them, Mr. Snyder. My sweet tooth is acting up again." Tolkien turned to look at the men. "Look at Simon Hardin. You are seeing your own death here today. If one of you so much as breathes a word of this, we will all meet our maker at the end of a rope. Mr. Snyder has put us all in great jeopardy this morning, but only we can put our necks in the noose. Do you understand that?"

The words were as cold and final as a judge's death sentence.

"Good," Tolkien said. "Now we will be on our way."

Gilfeather said, "Ain't we going to bury him?"

"The prairie will bury him in time. The prairie has time, Mr. Gilfeather, and we don't."

CHAPTER 11

RUNS TOWARD WATCHED as the hangman's knot sailed over the wide-spreading limb of the cottonwood tree. The noose drifted toward the ground and then jerked short above his head.

The young Cree blinked, and the rope disappeared, only to reappear a moment later soaring over the limb and drifting down like the roller-coaster flight of a magpie. The rope jerked to a stop, bouncing in the air with the shock of its abrupt stop.

Runs Toward blinked and the rope disappeared, reappearing a moment later as it soared over the limb and fell, noose wide and embracing, toward his neck.

Each time the scene repeated itself, the noose fell closer. Each time, Runs Toward came one step closer to death.

The young cowboy wanted to run, to flee the rope thrown by unknown assailants, but he seemed bound in place. He twisted in his blankets, grunting with the effort. The rope soared over the limb, falling toward him, noose opening to take him by the neck, to squeeze the life from him.

"No!"

Runs Toward rolled over, throwing his blankets free with a wide sweep of his arms. He was sweating, but the night was cold, and as wakefulness seeped into him, he shivered.

The sun was just beginning to paint the night gray, whispering its forthcoming dawn. The sound would grow until the light cracked the horizon with a crescendo of color.

Runs Toward pulled on his boots and stood, stretching, willing his consciousness to take away the dream, but it hung on him like death. He leaned against the cottonwood, fingers seeking clues in the rough bark, seeking to read the magic of the tree, to end his dreams. But he felt only the rough bark, the creaking of limbs moving to embrace the wind as the joints of an old man might grate together on a rainy day.

The young Cree's vision swept the graying prairie, watching for movement, for the long shadows that would signal a four-legged animal and meat. He would awaken Jimmy in a few moments and try once again to find game.

The dry summer winds were upon the plains, guzzling watering holes in great drafts. Prairie animals were seeking streams and green grasses in sheltered river bottoms, places protected from the summer sun. Grasses were browning in the heat, baking brittle in the sun. Only under the tree, in the shade and shelter and magic it offered, was the grass green still and soft.

Runs Toward's eyes rolled toward the east, and as the night stepped tentatively into day, he could see a spider at work on a nearby sage, spinning a web silver in the soft light. Later the sun would paint the web gold, and flies would tangle themselves in that finely spun trap.

The young Cree thought for a moment about Eli Gilfeather, wondering if he had been caught in a golden web when he agreed to trade rustlers' money for his honor. All Eli had wanted was independence and security. An elusive combination.

Runs Toward took a washcloth and stepped toward the spring, eyes seeking any rattlesnakes that might have come in the night to hunt mice. None slithered away from his step or rattled defiance at his intrusion, but that time would come. Rattlesnakes had no less need for food than the Wilders did, and they would follow the mice to the spring. When the Little Brothers came, he would ask their forgiveness for killing them.

He knelt beside water glowing in the first rays of the sun,

and dipped his washcloth into it. He draped the wet cloth across his face, feeling its coolness. Water dripped from it, catching on his chest and tracing icy rivulets on skin warming with the touch of sun. Runs Toward scrubbed his face, the back of his neck, his chest, and his arms, preparing himself for the sanctity of the day. Washing away the sweat from his dream.

For a while he had not dreamed of death. Now the dreams returned, but they were different. No longer did he run toward his death: He had found it. Each night the noose dropped closer. Each night he came one step closer to feeling the rough hemp around his neck.

The flap opened on the makeshift tent Runs Toward and Jimmy had pitched, and Jimmy stepped into the morning, hair gold in the early sun. He walked away from the tent, turning his back on the camp to relieve himself. Then he returned, collecting buffalo chips, striking a match against his thumbnail to light the morning fire.

The Wilderses had long since used all their coffee, but tea, rationed until it barely colored the water, still covered the bottom of a glass jar brought from Nebraska.

Jimmy knelt beside Runs Toward and the Cree handed him the washcloth. The boy scrubbed himself clean, rinsed the cloth, squeezed it almost dry, and stepped away to the tree, hanging the cloth over a low-hanging branch.

Only then did the two speak.

"West?" The word fell flat from Jimmy's mouth.

North, south, west: The direction didn't seem to matter, except that they would not hunt east because they would be blinded by the rising sun. Beyond that proscription, finding game was a matter of chance, chance growing less by the day.

"Doesn't make much difference."

"I have a feeling we might run into something out west."

"Could be."

The two squatted on the prairie, feeling the sun on their shoulders, enjoying the silence.

"Jimmy?"

"Yeah."

"Do you think your mother would let me take all of you back to Fort Benton in the wagon?"

The boy shook his head. "Have to wait for Pa."

"What if I took you to Fort Benton, and I came back here to wait?" The next words came soft and spare. "I have to be here, anyway."

"Why?"

"Waiting to see some people."

Jimmy stood and stretched. "Nope. Ma wants to be here when he comes back. Rosie and me, too."

There was no doubt in the boys's voice, no compromise. Runs Toward wondered how there could be so little doubt in a twelve-year-old's mind. He turned to stare at Jimmy and saw—

Runs Toward blinked and turned away, but this time the image remained, carried him back to the day of the hanging. Now, now in the soft light from the east, Runs Toward could see the dead man's face superimposed on Jimmy's. The forehead, the stubborn chin, the nose. Eyes set brooding under bushy brows, and a sense of wonder on his face.

The dream. He was dreaming again in daylight—but no, this was no dream. Runs Toward could see the man's face on Jimmy's because . . . The Cree's widening eyes swept around the little camp. A woman, a boy, and a girl. He resisted the images, but they were stronger than his resolve: mounted men, visages grim and black and white as skulls, surrounding a pleading man dressed in a plaid flannel shirt and coarse wool pants.

The words rang in Runs Toward's ears until they seemed to peal across the prairie like the bells of a church. *Tell my wife that I love her. Tell my children that I love them, that I didn't mean to leave them alone. Please . . . you must find them for me.*

Spread before him in this tableau of desperation was the family of the man he had helped to hang. Runs Toward saw his guilt written on Jimmy's face, on the nose and chin and forehead so much like his father's.

The man had been innocent; his weeping railed at the injustice of life, at the pain his death would inflict on his family.

Runs Toward leaped to his feet. He didn't remember the first step, or the second, or the third. He didn't remember when he realized that he was running. He felt only his compulsion to run into the blinding light of the morning sun, his feet barely touching the prairie grasses.

Runs Toward could feel the heat of the sun on his face, and he expected that he would curl into a fine, white ash as he neared the horizon. He saw only the sun, his stumbling feet feeling their way past sagebrush and rock.

Jimmy watched wide-eyed as Runs Toward ran into the sun and disappeared, crying a plaintive "No-o-o-o-o!"— wild and lonely as the call of a wolf.

Runs Toward stopped, hands on his knees, gasping for breath. The run sucked the air from him as the sun had sucked the darkness from the prairie, feeding on it, burning brighter and brighter in the morning air.

Runs Toward stood, breath rattling in his lungs. He shielded his eyes with his hand and stared against the light of the sun. He was looking for an indentation in the grass, a crushed prickly pear, anything that would mark the long-ago passing of a wagon, one horse, and four people.

In the end, his nose told the tale. The scent was faint now, after more than a month of drying in the sun, after a month of visits by predators. But still the sickly sweet smell of old death lay on the prairie. Somewhere between here and the wagon trail they would have been following that scent was rising from the earth.

Had Runs Toward been a prairie wolf or a coyote, he

could have followed his nose to the kill. That track had been followed many times by scavengers over the past month. But Runs Toward was not a wolf or coyote. He was a man trying to track his destiny by reading faint signs on the Montana prairie.

The scent grew stronger as he neared, and then he saw the carcass, hide painted black in silhouette, painted black by a carpet of flies gathered for the rancid feast. The stench was nearly unbearable as he neared.

Coyotes had opened the horse's belly and torn at the soft organs they found inside. After days and nights of heat had softened the animal's flesh, they had tugged at the meat around the animal's haunches, tearing sustenance from death.

White ribs poked now into the morning sun, and the hide around the horse's skull stretched tight over bones poking sharply into the prairie. Eye sockets were empty and staring.

Runs Toward hesitated, reluctant to step any closer to this obscenity of death, but he forced himself closer, hand covering his mouth and nose. When the flies rose in a black cloud that threatened to cover him, to crawl across his face with their stench-laden legs, he almost ran, but he had to know.

He walked closer, stopping within touching distance— and there, on the animal's right shoulder, was the pitch-fork brand, etched in death as in life. There was little difference between the pitchfork and Old Man Tolkien's trident. An honest mistake could be made between the two, an honest mistake that took one man's life and left his wife and children helpless on the prairie, an honest mistake that had made a young Cree cowboy into a murderer.

Runs Toward's gut contracted with the proof of his complicity in Samuel Wilders's death, with the stench of death that surrounded him. His gut emptied then.

*   *   *

The Wilderses stood in a little knot, watching him walk toward them. Runs Toward seemed weary, clumsy on the earth, as though he had lost his grace since running into the sun. They watched him now as a band of deer would watch the approach of a predator, trying to gauge their fate in the quickness of step, to read intent in the way the approaching figure held his head.

When he neared the Wilderses stood silently, trying to read the young man's face. He avoided their gaze, watching his feet instead as they parted drying grasses on the prairie.

He walked to the spring, where he stripped off his shirt and tossed it in a heap on the grass. He kneeled then, shaking his long black hair into the spring, leaning forward until his head was totally submerged. He remained there until it seemed that he must be dead, and then he reared back, water spraying from his hair.

Runs Toward gasped, sucking air into his empty lungs, and then he plunged again into the pool, burying his body in the water head to waist. The water bleached his body gray, and it seemed that the life had left it. Only a few tiny bubbles rose as his ears and nose filled with the cooling water. Then he exploded from the pool, chest heaving as though he had been running for a very long time. He stood, deep breaths racking his body.

Still the Wilderses stood in silence, watching this scene played out, trying to read the theme in this strange pantomime.

Runs Toward kicked a small pile of buffalo chips into the ring of stones that marked the family's outdoor fireplace, feeding the fire warming the blue enamel coffeepot. Then he walked to his war bag, hanging from a rope slung over a tree branch, and took out a clean pair of trousers and a new shirt. He stepped into the enclosure where the Wilderses slept, and emerged a moment later wearing fresh clothing.

The scent of burning wool curled into the air as he dumped his soiled clothing on the burning buffalo chips. He stood for a moment, watching as yellow tongues of flame rose to taste this new offering, to be sure that the fire was consuming the stench of the long-dead horse.

Runs Toward returned to his war bag, taking a small beaded deerskin bag from it. He removed silver leaves from the bag, placing them on a sandstone rock and touching a match to them. The scent of burning sage filled the air, and Runs Toward waved the smoke over his body, cleansing himself spiritually as he had cleansed himself physically.

Cree words, rusty with disuse, spilled over Runs Toward's tongue and into the total silence of the Wilder camp, and then the young Cree crossed himself, memories of his youth mixing in this strange ritual.

Only then did he acknowledge the Wilderses. He stepped up to Sarah and reached toward her, palms up. She took his hands, and he led her toward the family's makeshift table, seating her at one side, taking a seat opposite.

His words came soft and low and compelling. "Tell me about your husband. Tell me everything you can remember about him."

A question crossed Sarah's face, and then she began to speak. The words came slowly at first, and then in a rush, as much catharsis as recollection. As she spoke, Jimmy and Rosie came to the table to sit down, to share their mother's view of their father before they were born.

"I first saw him on the boardwalk in front of the Friendly Mercantile. He had come up from Texas with one of the trail herds, and he had been paid and was cut adrift, spending a few days 'amidst folks,' as he put it, before going back to Texas.

"He was handsome then, still is. He wasn't much older than I—I was sixteen, and shy, terribly shy. I remember that he stared at me, just stood there with his hat in hand and stared at me as though I were the most remarkable thing he had ever seen.

"I had been there for a good twenty minutes, and when I made my purchases, he stepped up and asked me if he could carry my things for me. The way he said it, it seemed that doing that little thing for me would be the most wonderful thing that ever happened to him."

Sarah Wilders, caught in her recollections, looked at her children and blushed. Rosie covered her mouth with her hand and giggled, and Jimmy looked across the prairie as though seeking game.

"He was so different from the farm boys around Friend. He seemed wild . . . and beautiful . . . the way that a white-tailed deer slipping through a copse of willows is beautiful, and a cow chewing its cud is so . . . well, plain. Maybe, that was why we fell . . . well. I don't know.

"Father and Mother were opposed at first. Said he had little to offer, but . . . I will never forget the way he looked at me. He saw something so special in me, and I wanted to be what I saw reflected in his eyes."

Sarah's hands fluttered on the table, and her eyes dropped to the rough-hewn table, as though she were reading notes in the rough swirls of the weathered wood.

"He tried hard to be a farmer, but . . . he never was. His being a farmer was like trying to tame a wild animal for a pet. They never get the wild out of them, never want to be caged. When he talked about coming out here, I saw how much he had given up for me, and I thought . . . well, we came."

Runs Toward interrupted the silence that followed. "What did he look like?"

"He isn't as tall as you. When I was standing on my toes, we were"—her hands fluttered again—"just about the same height. Jimmy favors his father; my parents said that from the first. He's handsome, like Jimmy will be."

Rosie broke in, "But I'm pretty as a picture. Mommy says I'm pretty as a picture."

Sarah smiled, "Yes, Rosie, pretty as a picture."

Rosie glowed, and then Sarah spoke again, "Samuel is a gentle man. All along the trail, he tried to do special things for me, bring me flowers, pick berries when he found some. He always treated me as though I were so special, and I tried so hard to be special for him."

Sarah raised her head, and stared into Runs Toward's eyes. "I miss him so. Even after we had lost everything else, I thought that somehow . . . Samuel had such high hopes, and he was such a hard worker, and I thought . . . then he disappeared, and I . . ."

Runs Toward reached across the table and took her hands. "I know." He stared into Sarah's eyes. "Did Samuel carry anything, anything that a person might notice if he saw him on the trail somewhere?"

"No, I . . . don't think so. He was dressed like pretty much everyone else."

"The tobacco pouch, Ma," Jimmy said.

"Oh, yes, the tobacco pouch. He carried that with him from Texas. It was leather, beaded. Beautiful, really, and it smelled of tobacco. I don't know how he came to have it, but he carried that with him always."

"No . . . Ma, I forgot. He traded it for a broken-bladed pocket knife he had. Someplace in Kansas."

"Yes, I suppose."

"Mrs. Wilder . . ." Runs Toward hesitated, and then the words came in a rush. "I have to leave for a few days. I have an idea where . . . your husband is—might be—and I want to see if . . . I can find him."

"No." Sarah Wilder pulled her hands away from Runs Toward. Her eyes turned toward the dugout, and she pushed her hands on the tabletop, struggling to rise, but the Cree grasped her wrists and held her.

"I have to go, Mrs. Wilders, but I'll be back. You won't

be left alone here again. I have something that I have to do, and I need your help. You have to take care of Jimmy and Rosie, here. You have food for a couple of days, and water.

"I've been holding out. I've got a can of peaches in my saddle bag. You can have that tonight as a kind of celebration."

Runs Toward held her hands, staring into her eyes. "I have to go. I need you to take care of your children. Please, Mrs. Wilders."

The woman sagged back in her seat. "Yes."

"I'm going, too," Jimmy announced.

"No, you have to stay here . . . in case a bunch of antelope wander near. Your mother needs you here, Jimmy."

Jimmy's face stiffened and then relaxed. He nodded.

Runs Toward spent the next fifteen minutes packing his gear. Once he was astride his horse, he stared down at Jimmy. "I'll leave one horse, and you have cartridges for your rifle." Then he added, "It's up to you now, Jimmy."

Jimmy nodded. It always had been up to him.

Runs Toward walked his horse to the spring, leaning down to pull the shovel free from the soil beside it. The blade made a sucking noise as it pulled loose from the wet earth.

"Why you taking that?" Jimmy asked.

Runs Toward turned to stare at the young boy. "Might need it to clear out a spring along the way."

He turned, and touched his heels to the mare's flanks. She stretched into an easy lope, disappearing across the prairie as the Wilderses watched, a tiny knot of humanity on a sea of Montana grass.

CHAPTER 12

THE HORSES STRETCHED out single file, each following the one before, each, with that sixth sense that horses seem to have, picking its way through the darkness and the grass and sage and rock carpeting the rugged hills above the Missouri Breaks.

Stars, dimmed by a sun the men could not yet sense, had retreated from the sky, leaving the earth in inky blackness, and as the men rode blindly, their other senses screamed for clues to find their place on the earth's surface.

Ears strained for the sound of wind moaning through ponderosa pine, or rustling through cottonwood leaves. They listened for the murmur of streams lapping against their banks, for the sound of a coyote telling the world where men weren't so they could discover where they were.

Any attempt to speak, to break the connection with creak of saddle leather and the jangle of bridles in front and behind, was greeted harshly, the harshness a gauge of the men's uncertainty.

They rode blindly forward, hands loose on the rains, each trusting his horse to find its way across the Montana prairie. Mixed with the uncertainty of the night was the uncertainty of what lay ahead. They rode on, straining their senses for a sign, listening for a signpost.

The Musselshell River emerged from the night, discernible not so much by the sounds of running water—the river moved tentatively as a bride toward its union with the Missouri—as by the rustle of cottonwood leaves, the gurgle of an occasional eddy, the thump of deer hooves moving away from man smell.

The scent of mint and rose danced through the cool night air, teasing the nose of horse and man alike. It was the Musselshell, all right. Knowing that eased the men's tension. They knew where they were. They knew they weren't lost forever on this darkened prairie.

Archie McDonald, scout for the vigilantes, nudged his horse's right shoulder with his knee, urging the animal toward the water, asking the horse in the subtle language of rider and bearer to pick its way down one of the shale ridges to the valley below.

The horse turned slightly, hesitating a moment before plunging off the valley's shoulder, triggering a rattle of cascading shale. Below, the slope was gentle, and the horse picked its way, ears pricking in the darkness as each of the mounts behind took the same path.

Below, the horses found a trail gouged into the valley floor by horses dragging cottonwood logs downstream to be cut up for passing river steamers. Archie's horse picked up speed then, his feet finding certain purchase in the old trail, his nose tasting the torn earth and dust.

The band continued until the night grayed toward day, until the sounds of moving horses behind McDonald translated into dark shadows in a shadowy world. One of the men split off the line then, and urged his horse to the front.

"How much farther?"

"Mile. Mile and a half, maybe."

"We'll stop here for a minute," Tolkien said, and McDonald nodded, reining his gelding to a halt. Tolkien wheeled his horse off the trail, waiting for the line to close up. The horses halted. The men turned expectantly toward him. Tolkien spoke, the words whispered into the night.

"We sent some boys out here this spring to tell Billy that he'd best be careful about the company he keeps. Couldn't find him. He's an old mountain man. Been in this country since the beginning, and he knows all the tricks when it comes to keeping out of sight. We're not going to give him that chance this morning.

"Billy has set himself up in an old fort, stockade and all. He'll be in the cabin with his woman. You watch out for her. She's Blackfoot, and she'd just as soon lift your hair as not.

"Soon as she figures out what we intend to do with her husband, she'll be on the prod. Some of you boys will have reservations about shooting a woman. Well, she's not white, and she won't have any qualms about shooting you. Keep that in mind.

"Could be some of Billy's rustler friends are in there with him. Just keep your heads down if the shooting starts, and we'll burn the cabin.

"That's it. Everyone from here"—Tolkien motioned in the near darkness with his hand—"will go around back with Archie. From here back, will come with me. Mr. Gilfeather, I want you up front with me.

"Let's go."

Billy Downs awoke in total darkness. He rolled from his bunk, favoring a back laced with arthritis from years of sleeping on cold, hard ground.

The old mountain man strained his ears, trying to make his mind understand what his nerves had felt. There it was again! The sound of bridled horses coming up on the cabin. Downs slipped to the door, reaching down to pick up his lever-action rifle. He peeked through the rifle slots in the cabin's heavy wooden shutters.

In the half light of false dawn, he saw them, a string of shadows black as death forming a semicircle in front of the cabin. Downs padded to the back of the cabin, bare feet padding silently on the rough wood floor.

California Ed's feet hit the floor as he muttered, "What the hell?"

"Hush," Downs said. "They've got us boxed in."

California Ed stepped to the door between the cabin's two rooms and picked up the rifle he'd propped there. He levered a shell into the chamber as silently as possible and left the rifle at full cock. He walked to a window and pressed his back to the heavy log wall for protection before leaning over to peer through the gun ports.

"They sure as hell do," he whipsered.

"Who is it?"

"Same as before, I suspect."

"Probably."

Downs stopped to take inventory. Meadowlark was gone. She hadn't said good-bye, just left in the night. She must be off tanning those buffalo robes. Soft as silk and warm as an August day, the robes were her specialty. She had some secret ingredient in the process that she refused to share even with her family. So when it was time to tan, she went off on her own. That might be it, and it might not. For nearly thirty-five years Downs and Meadowlark had lived together and still he didn't know her, not really. But it was good that she had gone. At least, she had slipped this trap. "Hidey-hole," he whispered.

"What?"

California Ed's question came from a deeper shadow inside the dark cabin.

"Got myself a hidey-hole," Downs said. "Beneath the counter. Little food and water. Last time they came, I dropped in there."

"Room for two?" California Ed asked.

"Don't know."

"Well, let's find out."

The two slipped into the other room, padding silently as bears.

A businessman had built the cabin in 1868 as a store-room and trading post for a fort at the mouth of the Mus-selshell. He thought that the wide valley at the junction of the two rivers was an amenable site for a town. That and the deeper waters in the Missouri below the Musselshell would give the fort a longer steamboat season and easier access than Fort Benton upstream.

Everyone except the Sioux agreed, but the Sioux held sway. That recalcitrant tribe didn't burn the fort, but they killed everyone they found near the buildings. Trade drifted away to safer climes.

Billy Downs had settled into the trading post, using one of the rooms for his and Meadowlark's bedroom and the other for his friend California Ed. The two cut wood from the cottonwood stands near the river to feed the boilers of the passing river steamers. When Montana entrepreneur T. C. Powers of Fort Benton stocked the post with trading goods, the little business thrived.

The vigilantes were about to put the post out of business unless the old mountain man could find a way out of the ambush.

A long counter divided California Ed's room. Hanging behind it were stocks of coffee and tobacco and flour and bacon and ammunition. Beneath the counter were barrels of whisky.

Downs slipped behind the counter, sliding a couple of empty boxes out of the way. He slipped the blade of his belt knife between the cracks in the rough plank flooring and tipped one of the planks up on edge. Beneath, scratched in the barren earth, was a shallow grave. At one end were a candle and a bottle of water, left there as though to light the way to the hereafter.

"Last time, I slipped in here. They didn't find me. Spent a day and night in that hole, wondering if they'd find it or if they'd torch the cabin. They didn't, but a day is a long time to spend in the dark like that, so this time I threw in the candle.

"Sons a bitches helped themselves to some coffee and tobacco. I could hear them down there, thumping around and prying into things that wasn't theirs. Took a little cask of whisky. Damn thieves. That's what they are. Sons a bitches."

California Ed whispered, "Billy, the both of us won't fit in there."

Downs stared into the hole. "No."

"They'll hang whoever they find in here."

"Yup."

"Billy, I don't want to hang. I purely do not want to dance my last jig at the end of a rope. I'd rather be burned alive, slow, the way the Sioux do it, than be hanged."

"I know. There's something god-awful about choking to death at the end of a rope."

"We'll fight."

"Too many of them, Billy. They'll kill us sure as hell."

"Going to kill us, anyway."

"One of us could hide. They don't know that two of us are in here."

"No, they don't."

"Well, how the hell are we going to decide?"

"Who lives and who hangs?"

"Yeah."

"We could flip a coin."

"That's a hell of a thing."

"Yeah."

The silence stretched for what seemed to be forever, and then Downs spoke. "You have any kids, California?"

"Did once. With a Shoshone woman. With her for damn near six—no seven—years. Little boy and girl, both of them bright as a June morning."

"What happened?"

"The pox. Killed them all. Damnedest thing."

Ed looked up. "What about you and Meadowlark?"

Downs shook his head. "You ever read the Bible, California?"

"No."

"I don't much, either, but there's one part in there that

talks about it being easier for a camel to go through the eye of a needle than for a rich man to go to heaven."

California nodded.

"Well, I always figured that Meadowlark made me so rich that if I was given even one more thing I wouldn't be able to go to heaven. She's one hell of a woman, California. She's more than I ever deserved."

"She's a good woman, Billy, and that's a fact."

"I've had a good life, California. Not many men get a chance to live like I did."

"Me, too."

"Hell, you've been a good friend, California. You squeeze down into that hole. No sense them killing the both of us. But one thing you've got to promise me . . ."

"Yeah?"

"You be sure that Meadowlark gets back up to her people. I'd hate to leave her here, at the mercy of those sons a bitches. And California?"

"Yeah?"

"Tell her, would you . . . Ah, hell . . . tell, her that I . . . well, you know." Downs's voice dropped to an almost imperceptible whisper. "Tell her . . . I love her, Ed."

It was California Ed's turn to stare at Downs. He sighed deeply before he spoke. "Ah hell, Billy. You crawl in the hole. Might be that they won't hang me. I don't count for much. Never did. Looking forward to the summer, but I wasn't wild about another winter up here. That cold gets into your bones, you never get it out."

Then the words boomed into the cabin, hollow and pounding as though the two men were standing inside a giant base drum.

"Hello, the cabin."

The two men looked at each other then, color draining from their faces. Downs stepped to a gun port in the front of the cabin and looked out.

The sun had painted the day in soft yellows and greens.

The grass atop the ridges surrounding the river valley shined golden as a communion cup, and the rustling leaves of the cottonwoods flashed.

"Come on out, Downs," the voice said. "It's time."

Downs squinted into the light, trying to put features on the black silhouettes outside. Tolkien. Old Man Tolkien was the one. He wondered for a moment if he could leave a message so Meadowlark would know what had happened. But then he shook off that thought. Nothing would be left of him when these men rode away, nothing at all.

"Go to hell," Downs yelled.

The words came with a dead man's resolve. Downs had accepted his fate. Tolkien could threaten him with nothing worse. He would fight to the death.

"Might as well come out, Billy."

"So's you can hang me?"

"We'll give you a fair trial."

Downs's chuckle came low and deadly. "Tied the knot yet?"

"Come on out, Billy, or we'll torch the cabin and sit off a ways and watch you roast alive. Let your wife out, Billy. We've got no argument with her. Being burned alive is a hell of a way to go. You don't want her to go like that."

Billy's eyes closed tight. If Meadowlark saw the smoke from the fire, she'd come running . . . , right into the cattlemen's guns.

A deep breath rattled into Downs's lungs. He turned and slouched through the cabin, stopping where California Ed waited at the window, listening as his fate was decided.

"California, if we fight, Meadowlark will hear the gunfire and come back. They'll kill her. She won't go easy, but they'll kill her. I can't fight 'em. It'd be the same as if I pulled the trigger on her. I'm sorry, California, but I just can't do that.

"So you climb down in the hidey-hole. Doubt they even

know that you're here. Then you can tell Meadowlark what I said."

"Hell, Billy, she knows how you feel about her. I see that in her eyes every day. You don't need me to tell her anything, and I ain't keen on seeing another winter. Let's get this over with, Billy."

California Ed grinned, the gesture twisted grotesquely on his face, and Billy Downs tried to grin back.

"You're a helluva man, California."

"You, too, Billy. I'm proud to have known you."

The two slipped the hammers on their rifles to half cock and propped them against the rough log walls. They shook hands, then, their grips firm and strong, and walked together to the front of the cabin.

"We're coming out, Tolkien. Let's get on with this trial."

Jick-Jack Snyder watched Billy Downs and California Ed step from the shadows of the cabin. His eyes were red and scratchy, because he'd hardly closed them since that day he killed Simon Hardin.

Jick-Jack didn't dare close his eyes; each time he did, he saw etched on the insides of his lids the gray and pink of young Hardin's exploding brain.

Jick-Jack lay awake at night, staring at stars that winked white and then yellow and then red through his blood-gorged eyes. He dared not even blink for fear that he would see again the surprise and the gore of that bloody moment.

And still worse than those images was the isolation. The cowboys were shunning Jick-Jack. No one spoke to him, no one singled him out for a word or a game of pitch by the light of the campfire. The cowboys' eyes dwelled on him for no more than a moment, as though they were afraid that any contact, even a glance, would contaminate them with his strange disease.

For most of the cowboys, the bunkhouse was the only

family they knew. They shared bad food and long days and brutal winters and life and death together. They shared the great adventure and the great cruelty of life, and that knitted each strand of their lives into a fabric that held them together.

Jick-Jack had been cut away from that crew, from his family. He was alone in the immensity of the Montana prairie with only the moan of the passing wind for company. He would have welcomed a curse, even a kick, any acknowledgment that he existed, but he was being shunned. Now Downs and Ed stood blinking in the bright light of the prairie morning. Downs shielded his eyes with his hand and stared up at Tolkien. "If this be a trial, tell me what I am charged with."

Tolkien spoke only one word, but that word came solemn as a death knell. "Rustling."

"Well, that's easy, then. I'm no rustler, so you all can go home."

"We'll decide that."

"No—you've already decided that, or you wouldn't be here."

"You'll get a fair trial."

"Pfaugh! I'd be treated better by the Sioux than you, and they hate my guts."

Silas Tolkien stood in his stirrups, putting his head just a little above the other riders. "Archie, you check out those horses in the corral. Get a list of brands." Tolkien hesitated a moment, and then his eyes found Jick-Jack. "You check out the cabin. Might be you can find a little whisky. We're likely to have worked up a thirst by the time this is finished."

Jick-Jack looked as though he had been granted redemption. "Yes, sir," he whooped, stepping down off his horse.

Downs snarled, "You'll damn well pay for any whisky you take from my post."

Tolkien ignored him. "You two," the old man said, pointing his quirt. "Check the outbuildings. See what you find. Watch for little hidey-holes. Billy knows all about hidey-holes."

Downs watched the men disappear and then turned his attention back to Tolkien. "What about California Ed? He ain't done nothing. He just cuts wood for me."

"That's enough."

"You son of a bitch."

Tolkien smiled. "I see that you and Mr. Gilfeather speak the same language. If we need a translator during the trial, perhaps we can impose on him. You know Mr. Gilfeather, do you not?"

Downs stared into Tolkien's face, seeking the message beneath the spoken words. Then realization spread across the old mountain man's face.

"Never heard of him."

"Having friends in high places might help you in your pleadings," Tolkien said. "Certainly, Mr. Gilfeather is in an elevated position."

"Not so elevated as I'm about to be, you son of a bitch."

Jick-Jack scurried from the cabin door. "Found some dried beef in there. Barrels of it."

Downs stared up at Tolkien. "Buffalo. It's dried buffalo."

"Mr. Downs, when was the last time you saw a buffalo down here?"

"About a month ago. An old bull. There's still a few in some rough country here about."

Tom Abby spurred his horse over from one of the sheds. "Hides in there. All salted down and ready to ship."

"Buffalo hides, Mr. Abby?"

Abby's left eye squinted shut, and he stared perplexed at Tolkien. "Buffalo hides? Spotted buffalo, maybe, but I've never seen a branded buffalo, and they all have brands on 'em."

"Any Trident brands?"

"Yes, sir."

"I buy hides," Downs said. "I don't pay much attention to the brands."

"You don't pay enough attention to the brands. That's certain enough. Well, now we know where the dried beef comes from."

"Ain't no dried beef. That's dried buffalo."

The men returned from the corral. One handed Tolkien a scrap of paper.

Tolkien studied the list for a moment before staring accusingly at Downs. "You don't pay much attention to the brands on horses either, do you, Mr. Downs?"

"I've got a bill of sale for every one of those horses. Inside on that shelf underneath the counter."

"Not worth the paper they're printed on."

Downs glowered. "I have a bill of sale. If the bills of sale are not legitimate, I have been defrauded. But I am no damn rustler. Even if I was a rustler, I wouldn't be half the thief you are, Tolkien."

Tolkien's words came in little more than a whisper. "The trial is over, Billy Downs. You are found guilty of rustling and consorting with known thieves."

The old man sat back in his saddle, pulling his attention away from the two men.

"Tie them up, boys. I'm about to pass sentence."

"Wait." Ryder Davis spurred his horse between the vigilantes and the two men about to be hanged. "It seems to me that Mr. Downs has raised some reasonable questions as to his guilt. I believe those questions should be addressed."

Tolkien looked at Davis without rancor; when he spoke, his voice was flat, emotionless.

"We don't have time for this, Mr. Davis."

"Two men's lives are at stake, sir—and our souls."

Tolkien's eyes squinted almost shut. "State your case. You've got five minutes, and then we'll get on with it."

Davis stood on the cabin's porch, holding a sheaf of paper in his hand.

"Mr. Downs clearly has a bill of sale for each of the horses in the corral," he said.

"How many of those bills of sale are notarized, Mr. Davis?" Tolkien asked.

"Two."

"Of seventeen?"

"Yes."

"There are two Trident horses in the corral. Were there notarized bills for the Trident horses?"

"No."

"The reason for that, Mr. Davis, is that rustlers stole those horses from Trident ranch."

"Can you prove that those horses were stolen . . . sir?"

Tolkien glowered at Davis. "How the hell am I going to prove that while I'm out here on the prairie and all my records are back at the place."

"That's my point, sir. We're miles from a notary public. Bills of sale are only seldom notarized."

"Mr. Davis," Tolkien growled, "I know those horses are mine. I know he has them. I know I didn't sell them to him. That's all I need to know."

Davis collected his thoughts and tried another approach. "We have established from company records that Mr. Downs bought those steer hides."

"Like hell!" Tolkien's voice rose. "All we have *established* is that the records *show* that Downs bought the hides. He's probably just pocketing the money he says he paid for them."

"You don't know that, sir."

"I know it to my own satisfaction, and that's all that counts here, Mr. Davis."

"Yes," Davis whispered. "That's all that counts here. But what about the dried buffalo?"

"That, sir, is no more dried buffalo than I am full-blooded Chinese. If that is buffalo meat trimmed from some mythical herd near here, where are the hides?"

Davis turned to Downs. "Mr. Downs, will you please tell us where the buffalo hides are."

Downs, hands tied behind his back, was thinking about Meadowlark, how her hair even now shone black as a raven's wing, her eyes bright as a magpie's. She must have taken the hides, but if he told the vigilantes that a witness was about, they would track her down and kill her, just as they were about to kill him. He couldn't do that. He couldn't risk his wife's life in this phony trial.

He turned to look at California Ed. "I'm sorry, California, but . . ."

California shrugged his shoulders and smiled. "I know, Billy."

"No," Downs said louder. "I can't tell you where those buffalo hides are."

"Well, that's it, then," Tolkien said. "I sentence . . ."

"Wait! Reasonable doubt. Certainly some of you must question whether this man is guilty?"

"Doesn't matter," Tolkien said. "I've got no doubts. I sentence Billy Downs and California Ed to be hanged by the necks until they are dead, and to be left hanging as a warning to any other rustlers around here."

Tolkien's heels slammed into his horse's belly like a gavel rapping on a court bench, and the men moved off to a copse of trees behind the cabin.

CHAPTER 13

THE COTTONWOOD STOOD in a grove of younger trees, the only survivor of a stand swept away in a flood fifteen years before. Cottonwood seeds that collected on the riffle had taken root. But in the shade of the one remaining tree, the saplings perished for want of sunshine. So this tree stood alone in a little clearing amidst new growth that reached now less than half of its height.

There was a sense of peace in the little clearing, the old cottonwood lending an air of majesty that diminished the problems of those who came there. Billy Downs and Meadowlark came on Sundays to their "church," he to read the Bible or any books he could pick up from the passing steamboats, she to sew and listen to the passing of the river.

The clearing had been special for Downs and Meadowlark, and California Ed had come along, tentatively at first, to share this place and their days together. This was a good place to pray and a good place to die.

Billy Downs and California Ed were preparing to die. They sat, hands tied behind them, bareback on horses from the trading post's corral. The vigilantes figured the two would slip easier from unsaddled horses than from saddled ones. Anyway, there seemed little reason to take the time to saddle two horses for such a short ride.

The vigilantes lined both sides of a corridor of death open front and back. Only Jick-Jack Snyder occupied the corridor with the men, his pistol raised to fire the shot that would send the horses running and the men to their deaths.

California Ed's lips were moving, the fingers of his

hands roving by memory down a string of imaginary rosary beads.

Old Man Tolkien suppressed a grin. California Ed would find little help from his prayers. God was not likely to listen to the supplications of a thief.

The old man was about to nod to Jick-Jack, pistol cocked and pointed in the air. A little nudge on the trigger, and the two horses bearing the two rustlers would spook, leaving their riders kicking as the rope choked the life from them.

Tolkien owned Jick-Jack now, body and soul. Being shunned was hell on cowboys. Tolkien had seen it more than once—most put a bullet in their brains or rode into the middle of a stampede, preferring the killing blows of the cattle's hooves to being ostracized.

Jick-Jack had had a taste of what it was to be shunned, to be dead while he was still alive. But Tolkien had offered the cowboy a reprieve, setting him a task that forced the others to acknowlege the young cowboy; the old man was telling them implicitly that the shunning was finished. The simple task of sending Jick-Jack into the cabin to search it made him a key player in the trial of the rustlers. Simple as he was, Jick-Jack understood that he had been reprieved. He understood the debt he had incurred. When Tolkien asked the cowboy to be the executioner, to take upon his own soul the death of these two miscreants, Jick-Jack did not hesitate a moment. Jick-Jack Snyder would do anything Tolkien wanted him to, any damn thing at all.

"Any last words?" Tolkien's question was dripping with sarcasm. "Well, if you've got nothing to—"

Downs interrupted, "I've got something to say. I've got something to say to you four-flushers."

Tolkien cocked an eye. Most likely this would be a foulmouthed diatribe. Still, last words were rare; death usually came by surprise on the Montana prairie. Mr. Downs's comments might be interesting.

Tolkien nodded. "Speak your piece, Mr. Downs."

The old mountain man took a moment to sweep the cottonwood trees with his eyes; his nostrils flared as he sipped their acrid scent. He took a deep breath then, and turned his attention to the vigilantes.

"Didn't think I'd ever go like this. In the early days, I thought my scalp would hang from a Sioux lance. But it was given to me to live beyond those times.

"I saw the coming and the going of the fur trade. I saw the first of the gold miners trickle into this state, walking edgy, waiting for an arrow to cut them short. Then came the buffalo hunters. I hated those sons of bitches—"

Tolkien broke in. "Mr. Downs, we have more pressing business than listening to your life history. Please speed it up."

Downs glared at Tolkien. "You boys are taking the rest of my life. You can damn well give me a few minutes of yours."

Tolkien crossed his arms. "Proceed, but know that I'll cut you off mid-sentence if you get too windy."

Downs turned his attention to the cowboys. "Pfaugh. You shoulda seen this country when I first came to her. Grass—you've never seen grass like that—and buffalo to feed the nation. This was a place to be then.

"You could get rubbed out for stepping into Sioux territory, building a fire too big, not being ready for a blizzard, not reading sign right. But being so close to death made life sweet as a spring flower."

Downs' face twisted into a grimace then, and for a moment it seemed that the old mountain man might cry. The cowboys shifted their eyes away from him, afraid to watch any display of emotion, afraid of coming to feel something for the man they were about to kill.

"But the miners tore at this land, poisoned her waters, and the buffalo hunters rubbed out the buffalo. But they was pikers compared to you boys. You boys are rubbing the soul of this country into the dirt."

Downs glowered at the men surrounding him.

"Greed. That's all it is. There was free grass, so you brought herd after herd into this country. But the cattle eat the grass down to nothing, and they scrub the prairie into dust with their hooves. Grass went into the hole in the ground with the buffalo.

"Only thing that greened up this spring was death camas. Cattle ate that and died. That's where those hides came from. An old buffalo hunter came through this spring, skinning out the poisoned cattle. I bought 'em, just like the records said, and I sure as hell didn't dry that bloating beef.

"You lost a lot of cattle to death camas, didn't you, Tolkien?"

The old man sat silently astride his horse, his face carved from granite.

"That's what I thought. I'll tell you one thing, Tolkien. I've lived in this country a lot longer than you have, and she won't put up with you much longer. She's poisoning your cattle, now, and if that don't work, she'll just rub you out.

"You worry about rustlers? Hell!" Downs growled. "You boys want to know why you're really here?"

Silence.

"Well, I'll tell you, anyway. Ranchers can't control the weather, can't control the drought. And they won't control the number of cattle on this land because of their own greed. So they've decided to kill people who take cattle that are going to die anyway.

"Pfaugh. You're a hell of a bunch for pure stupid. Selling your souls for a few extra dollars and your boss's greed."

Downs leaned over the neck of his horse and spat.

"Get on with your dirty work, you sons a bitches."

Tolkien's face glowed a dull red. He spoke through gritted teeth. "You have anything enlightening to say, Mr. California Ed?"

California Ed shook his head.

"Well, let's get on with it, then."

Meadowlark threaded her way through the willow and rose thickets lining the banks of the Musselshell. This was Sioux country, but she was Blackfoot. Her people's country backed into the Rocky Mountains. The Blackfeet had the mountains at their backs and the plains at their feet. They hunted elk and deer and bear across rocky mountain slopes in the summer, sipping air redolent with life. They ventured on the plains in the fall to kill the buffalo, to show the other tribes why they were considered the fiercest of peoples.

Meadowlark lived away from her magic mountains because the man she loved lived here. He was a good man. He treated her better than a Blackfoot warrior would have. She had status here, not only among her own people, but also among the other Indian peoples. She lived very well, with all the cloth and beads and meat any person could want.

But sometimes she longed for the mountains, and she would ride then along game trails bordering the Musselshell, and she would smell the mint and the rose. She would listen to the rustling of the cottonwood trees and imagine them to be quaking aspen, and she would think of the carefree days of her youth.

Her packhorse carried fine buffalo robes, from the hunt that spring. Meadowlark didn't know why that one small herd of buffalo had chosen not to go underground with the others, but she was glad they remained to share their tongues and humps and flesh, to share their hides.

She would make a fine winter robe for Billy Downs. He would be warm, and when visitors came to the trading post, they would marvel at what a fine coat Billy Downs's wife had made for him.

Meadowlark would drop her eyes in modesty then, she thought, but Billy Downs would look at her and smile. Even now, after all these years, the thought of that secret smile put a shiver down her back.

Meadowlark kicked her horse into a trot, tugging her packhorse behind. She was only a short distance from the trading post, and her man would be wondering about her.

Caution was as much a part of Meadowlark's life as Billy Downs was. She stopped at the edge of the clearing to survey the trading post. No smoke swirled from the cabin chimney.

She saw the hoofprints of a large body of horses, marking the grass in front of the cabin. Perhaps the horse thieves had come to trade. Meadowlark smiled. She held horse thieves in high regard.

She slipped from the back of her horse and led him to the corral, hanging the bridle and saddle over the lodgepole railing. She opened the gate and slapped his haunches, urging him inside. She unloaded the packhorse, draping the buffalo hides over the fence. The sun would do them good. The sun did everything good.

The packhorse followed the others into the corral; Meadowlark carried a bucket of oats from a nearby shed to each of her two, holding the bucket safe from the other horses.

Concern nagged at her as she walked to the cabin. No one was inside. Perhaps her husband had gone looking for her, afraid that she had slipped off with a Blackfoot brave come courting. Meadowlark grinned. That was an old joke between Billy Downs and her.

Her walking stick, cut from an elder in her people's country, leaned against the door frame. She took it as she set out to study these tracks, to read in them the story of her missing husband.

Meadowlark heard then the nicker of a horse down by the river, in their special place. A smile spread across her face. Billy Downs was waiting for her in their reading and sewing place. He had seen her coming and was waiting for her.

Her husband Billy Downs was a great hunter and a great warrior, and she should have known that she could not sneak up on him unannounced. She walked toward the river then, her face alight with a smile. She would tell him that she had run away with a handsome Blackfoot brave and that she had come back only to steal his horses. He would be fierce; he would growl, and they would wrestle together, and then, maybe . . .

Her pace picked up as she walked toward the little clearing under the cottonwood tree, and then she saw the horsemen. Billy Downs and his friend California Ed stood between two lines of horsemen. They had ropes around their necks, and one horseman waited behind them with his pistol in the air, waiting to fire the shot that would send her husband to his death.

Meadowlark's eyes blurred with tears. She began to sprint toward the men, slipping through the trees silent as a wraith.

"Aiieee!" Meadowlark charged into the clearing, her braids flying behind as she ran to save her husband. She swung her walking stick like a Blackfoot coup stick, and she counted coups on her enemies this day.

"Aiieee!" She passed through the line of horses, thumping her staff into the ribs of startled vigilantes.

She broke through the line and into the aisle where Billy Downs and California Ed awaited their death. She saw the scene through tear-blurred eyes, but she ran on, one woman with a stick against an army of vigilantes. One woman bent on saving her husband.

Her mind seemed to be operating in flashes and clicks. She saw the rope draped around her husband's neck, saw where the other end was tied to the trunk of a nearby tree. If she could reach that rope and cut it, perhaps he could escape. Even with his hands tied behind his back, with the cut rope still around his neck and trailing behind the horse, he might escape.

Meadowlark might have reached the ropes, but for Jick-Jack's arm.

Jick-Jack's arm ached from holding his pistol upright through Billy Downs's speech. His soul ached with the responsibility of being the executioner in this peaceful little glade. When the walking stick cracked into his ribs with a satisfying thump, the muzzle swung around, and he pulled the trigger.

The bullet shoved Meadowlark back, and her eyes glazed. She tried to maintain her balance, tried to step forward one more time, tried to deliver just one more blow, but the second bullet struck her forehead. She wilted onto the prairie, falling in a loose coil on the earth.

Time stopped, the sound of the shots pressing against the ears of the cowboys as though the echoing would never stop, and then came the "No!" rattling from Billy Downs's throat. The old man's face was a tragic mask, his word rolling from his mouth like the sound of a drum marking an execution. *"Damn you all to hell!"*

Downs raised his heels then and brought them down hard against his horse's ribs. The vigilantes heard the mare grunt from the blow, from the effort of moving her bulk into a gallop, from the effort of shedding her rider to the care and comfort of a hangman's noose.

And then, even before the noose jerked tight to squeeze the life from Billy Downs, California Ed kicked his horse. "Wait for me, Billy—"

Ropes creaked with the weight of the swinging bodies, and the earth thumped with the sound of running horses, hollow as a drumstick beating against a loosened drumhead. Only that, and silence.

* * *

Runs Toward's body ached with each step of his horse, with the weight of the guilt that pressed him inexorably toward the earth. He stared at his horse's mane as he rode, glancing up only occasionally to take his bearing, avoiding looking at the rock outcroppings, afraid that his mind might etch Samuel Wilders's face there.

His destination lay ahead, a thin dark line on the prairie horizon marking the trees that followed the course of Crazy Woman Creek. It was there that he would find Samuel Wilders's body, or what remained of it.

It was a paradox that cottonwoods, trees that marked the course of water and life across the prairie, had become instruments of death. Now Runs Toward could see the break in the trees where the creek disappeared along the hillside. The tops of the trees seemed nothing more than shrubbery on the little hill. Below that shrubbery, he would find Wilders's body, if a passerby had not already done Runs Toward's work for him.

The prairie was beginning to break up now into little swales and rivulets and gullies and coulees that fed the creek below. Runs Toward found a deer trail leading along a juniper-tangled coulee to the creek below. He tried to remember if they had followed this trail that day so long ago, but his mind had been on other matters then. He had blindly followed where destiny led.

The mare tugged at the reins, anxious to reach the bottom of the hill, anxious to reach water. Runs Toward eased his hands on the reins, and she bounced down the slope, he standing to take the shock of her gait with his legs.

The creek bottom was more mosquito-infested swamp than anything. The hooves of hundreds of cattle seeking water and green grass had pocked the prairie gumbo, torn it until it bled brown into the creek, and then the cattle had moved on, seeking always tender green grass.

Runs Toward ground-reined the mare, untied the shovel

from the saddle, and followed a game trail upstream, leaving the horse to find shreds of grass left behind by the cattle.

The young Cree stepped around a shale wall on the hillside. When he saw the hanging tree, he jerked back. The hanging had run through his mind so long that Runs Toward wasn't sure where the dream stopped and reality began. But the stench had never been part of his dreams.

The young man's throat spasmed, and he almost lost his breakfast. He stopped, leaning against his knees, eyes focused on the trail in front of him before he looked again at the tree.

Samuel Wilders's body had given up its fight with gravity and coyotes tugging at the heels of the hanging corpse. Only Wilders's head still defied the pull of gravity. A little gust of wind spun it slowly at the end of the rope.

Thump! Thump! Thump! The rounded bottom of the shovel pounded into the little mound of earth beneath the tree. Sweat ran into Runs Toward's eyes as he shaped the mound, willing the earth to harden so passing coyotes would not dig up the remains, so Samuel Wilders finally would stay buried and out of the young man's dreams. *Thump! Thump! Thump!*

Next he stepped to a pile of sandstone that had broken off above and skittered down the shale wall lining Crazy Woman Creek. He used his shovel to pry up flat slabs of rock and carried the rocks to the grave, fitting the stones together in a patchwork of protection for Samuel Wilders's body.

He burned the last coil rope because he didn't want the grave to be associated with a hanging. No one should think that Wilders had been hanged because he was a rustler.

One stone, covered green and blue with lichen, he carried to a log beside the fire. Runs Toward sat, laying the weight of the stone on his thighs. With a sharp-edged rock, he began cutting into the stone, grinding the sharp face of one rock into the flat of the other.

The cutting took most of the day, Runs Toward stopping only when his hand ached too much to continue. He wanted the grooves deep so that they wouldn't easily disappear, so people would know who lay here in this little swale along muddied and bloodied Crazy Woman Creek. At the end, he blew the last of the dust from the grooves cut in the rock and looked at his handiwork.

Samuel Wilders
Died June 1884

Runs Toward set one edge of the tombstone deep in the soil, stomping the dirt firmly around it. As he worked, he thought of what he had yet to do.

Jimmy cocked his head, the way he always did when he pondered a problem. He had picked that up from his father, Sarah Wilders thought.

"Do you think he'll come back?" Jimmy asked his mother.

The boy's face was dusty and sweat-streaked from a day of hunting, another day with no game spotted.

"Yes, I think he'll be back," she said.

"Why?"

"He left his horse."

Jimmy considered that and then nodded. "S'pose he'll find Pa?"

"I hope he will."

The two were sitting across from each other at the table. Flies buzzed around them, finding more scent than sustenance on plates scrubbed clean by the family's hunger.

Sarah Wilders was emerging still from her deep depression, unfolding as a butterfly unfolds its wings after emerging from a cocoon.

"Ma?" Jimmy's question came in a whisper. "What do you suppose happened to Pa?"

"I don't know, Jimmy. I . . . know that he would be here if he could. At first, I thought that he had left us the way all of the other things did, like Grandma's dresser and Grandpa's shotgun and . . . all the other things.

"But your father wouldn't abandon us. I know he wouldn't."

Sarah wrung her hands, examining them as though seeing their dexterity for the first time. "I don't know why he hasn't come home, Jimmy. I know he would if he could."

Jimmy's voice almost disappeared into the evening air. "Do you think he's . . . Do you think he . . ."

Sarah raised her eyes to stare into Jimmy's. The boy's eyes glittered with tears, and she could see in him a younger Jimmy, the child he had been before this trip had laid so much responsibility on his young shoulders.

"Do you think he died, Ma?" Jimmy's face broke up, distorted by the tears in her own eyes.

"Jimmy, I don't know what else would keep him from us."

Sarah Wilders stood, eyes darting about the darkening prairie. "I think this country just swallowed him up and left us here alone. I used to think this land was evil, but it isn't that. It's just that it's so big . . . and we're so small."

Jimmy stood, walking on shaky legs toward his mother, tears streaming down his cheeks. She took him in her arms for the first time in years.

His fierce independence had driven him from her embrace at too early an age. But now he leaned against her, his tears soaking through her dress to her shoulder, his silent sobs shuddering against her as though he were freezing to death on this warm summer night.

"What are we going to do, Ma?"

"I don't know, Jimmy. We'll wait for Mr. Runs Toward, and then we'll decide."

"Do you like him?"

"Mr. Runs Toward?"

Jimmy nodded into his mouther's shoulder.

"Yes, I think I do."

"Like Pa?"

Sarah Wilders took Jimmy by the shoulders and held him at arm's length. "No, Jimmy, not like Samuel."

"I like him, too, but not like Pa."

"Your father was special." The moment the words left her mouth, Sarah Wilders realized that she was speaking of her husband as though he were dead. She pulled Jimmy to her then, and her own tears spilled into his hair.

They clung to each other as light fled the prairie, and darkness crept upon the land.

CHAPTER 14

"CHILLY."

"Yeah."

"Not long till daylight now."

"No."

"Will they put up a fight?"

"Why the hell wouldn't they?"

"Billy Downs didn't put up a fight."

"I know. I can't figure that out. Billy was a fighter."

"You knew him?'

"Sure."

"What he said, was it true?"

"What do you mean?"

"About cowmen ruining the land?"

Ryder Davis shoved his hat back on his head, the gesture lost to the darkness of the night and to Eli Gilfeather. The two men sat on a ledge above the Missouri, the river winking starlight at them from below.

"Couldn't be any other way."

"What do you mean?"

Davis tipped his head back to stare at the stars, bright still in the night air.

"Suppose your horse threw you out on the prairie, and you broke your leg."

"No horse could ever throw me."

"Ain't a horse that can't be rode. Ain't a man that can't be throwed."

"Not me."

"Yes, well. Just suppose that your cinch broke, and—"

"I keep my equipment in top shape."

"Eli, do you want me to answer the question or do you want to argue?"

"Sorry. Just a little nervous, that's all. Stringer Jack isn't going to be the pushover that Billy Downs and California Ed was and . . ."

"And the woman. Don't forget the woman, Eli."

"Don't worry. I'll never forget her, and I'll never forget what Jick-Jack did—"

"Wasn't Jick-Jack. Old Man Tolkien was pulling the strings, and Jick-Jack was just dancing."

Eli sighed. "Yeah, I know all about Tolkien pulling strings. Well, all right, let's say I get throwed."

"And you break a leg."

"And I break a leg."

"And your horse runs off."

"Not the way I train my horses. They wouldn't—"

"And your horse runs off."

"All right, my damn horse runs off. Never liked that piebald son of a bitch anyhow."

Davis chuckled. "Right. That piebald son of a bitch runs off. Well there you are on the prairie with no food or water and a broken leg."

"Think they can hear us talking?"

"If I thought they could, would I be talking?"

Eli considered that for a moment and then continued. "All right. I'm on the prairie with a broken leg and no food or water and that son of a bitch piebald has run off."

"Right. Well, there you are. The first day is bad. Your leg swells up and you can't even hobble along, but you know that you have to find water or you're a goner, so you start crawling along the prairie, dragging your leg behind you.

"You ever broke any bones, Eli?"

"Do you think I'm a kid? Course I have."

"Well, you know how it hurts worse the second day and the third?"

"Yeah."

"Well, that's how it is with you, out on the prairie. Your leg is hurting like hell. Your throat feels like somebody sprinkled sand all over it, and your backbone is rubbing a hole in your belly. Just about the time you're ready to give up the ghost, you come to this little swale on the prairie like that. . . . You ever see that huge cottonwood that grows all by itself out on the prairie?"

"Yeah, ain't that the strangest thing?"

"Yes. Anyway, this swale is like that. Kind of magic, somehow, and you crawl down into it because it has soft grass and some shade. You crawl into the shade and fall asleep.

"Well, when you wake up, you see these strange mushrooms growing around you. You don't know if they're poison or not, but you know you're going to die anyway if you don't get something working in your gut. So you nibble just a bit of the mushroom and fall asleep again.

"The second time you wake up, you feel great. You get up and walk around, feeling better than ever. You feel so good that you don't even notice your leg isn't broken anymore, not until you're watching the sun slip beneath the horizon."

"I'm not much for fairy tales, Ryder."

"Hear me out. . . . So you feel just great, not hungry or tired or sore or anything. All the cactus stuck in you from crawling across the prairie is gone. You're just on top of the world. "Well, along comes your piebald. All contrite about the trouble he's caused you, and come back to set it right."

"I'd shoot the son of a bitch."

"You can't."

"Why the hell not?"

"Your rifle's with your saddle. Remember, your cinch broke."

"Then I'd cut his throat."

"Then you'd walk all the way back to town."

"What town?"

"What difference does that make?"

"Okay, I'd go back and get my saddle. Wouldn't leave it on the prairie just because it has a broken cinch."

"All right, you go back and get your saddle."

"Well, then, I'd have my rifle, and I'd shoot that son-of-a-bitch piebald."

"Eli Gilfeather, you are one contrary son of a bitch."

"Just like that piebald."

"All right. Let's say you don't shoot it and you go into Fort Benton. There's a man who loves piebalds and you trade him off for a great horse. To celebrate, you go into the nearest bar to have a drink. There's a gambler there in the last stages of consumption. He's near death, and he tells you how he'd like to go back to Georgia to his family's plantation and get his life straightened around, but the doctor says he'll never survive the trip. You're standing there at the bar and you reach in your shirt pocket for two bits and find that mushroom you picked the day before. You feel sorry for the gambler, so you tell him to eat a little bit of that mushroom and go upstairs and go to sleep.

"Well, the next morning that gambler's the healthiest man you've ever seen. He's strutting around telling everybody about this magic mushroom you've got. He's so grateful that he slips you a hundred dollars in gold.

"Isn't long before there's a whole line of people waiting to take a bite of that mushroom, and every one of them eager as hell to slip you five double eagles. After a while you have five thousand dollars."

"Five thousand dollars?" the words came whispered. "Whoo-ee! I'm rich. Runs Toward and me will be able to start our ranch."

"Runs Toward, that Indian kid?"

"My son. Well, like my son." Suspicion edged into Gil-feather's voice. "How is it you know about Runs Toward?"

"Eli, never mind. Suppose you run out of mushroom. So you sneak back to that swale, careful as can be. You figure this time you'll take five mushrooms, make enough money to live in luxury in San Francisco. But as soon as you step off your horse, in ride five hardcases and start picking mushrooms.

"You tell them to stop, that there's enough mushrooms for everyone. But they're poking mushrooms into a bag fast as they can. You tell them that if they pick all the mushrooms, there won't be any more, but they keep picking.

"So what do you do?"

"Pick some more myself."

"Damn right. Mushrooms are going to be gone anyway. So you figure you might as well get your share. Before long, there isn't a single mushroom in that patch, and there never will be again.

"That's the way it is with the cattlemen, Eli. They're all trying to get their share of the mushrooms. If one stops, somebody else will just take his share. They're killing the range just like Billy said. Only place you find grass is where there isn't water, because cattle can't go long without water. Wherever there's water, there's no grass.

"And everybody's racing to get his share before all the mushrooms are gone. Every year more herds come in. Range is already overloaded, but they won't stop. Can't stop, any more than a kid could help picking up a nickel he found on the street."

Eli sighed. "Don't like to be part of anything like that."

"Do you like being part of a hanging party, Eli?"

"No, I sure as hell don't. I hate to think about what's going to happen when it turns light."

"Think they'll point the finger at you, Eli?"

Gilfeather stiffened. "What do you mean?"

"Tolkien told me to keep an eye on you. Said I should shoot you if you try to get away."

Eli's voice almost disappeared in a scratchy whisper. "Would you do that?"

"No," Davis said. "Would you run off and leave me to deal with Tolkien?"

"No."

"Didn't think so."

"Why'd he pick you?"

"He figures that he and I are peas in a pod."

"You and Tolkien? The old man's gone daft."

"No, there's something to what he thinks. He and I are both rich."

"You as rich as Tolkien?"

"Maybe more."

"Then what the hell are you doin' out here?"

"Blood."

"You kill somebody?"

Davis chuckled low in his throat. "No, I didn't kill anybody. I meant that I have a little wildness in my blood."

"Oh."

Davis shifted his weight, trying to find a more comfortable position. Only after he found it did he speak. "Eli, how many store clerks and bartenders have you seen in your life?"

"A lot."

"You ever see a rich one?"

"No."

"Clerks don't get rich. You know who gets rich?"

"I sure as hell don't."

"Rustlers get rich. They aren't always called rustlers. Sometimes they're called pirates and sometimes business-men, but they're all rustlers just the same. To get rich, you have to be willing to take risks—along with everything else you can get your hands on.

"My great-great-grandfather was a pirate. He made a fortune at it. My father ran the blockade during the Civil

War. He knew which way the war was going, so he wouldn't take any of that Southern scrip. He took cotton and gold. Cotton was at a premium in the North, so he played one side against the other and made a fortune. Hell, he's rich as Croesus. My father was a rustler, Eli, . . . and I am, too. It's in the blood."

"I don't believe that!"

"Eli, if I'm not a rustler, would you tell me how the hell I know that you are?"

Eli sucked in his breath. "This is all a trick, isn't it? Tolkien set you on me so he could get proof, so he could hang me? You rotten son of a bitch."

"Twenty dollars, Eli."

"Is that what he paid you?"

"No, that's what Stringer Jack paid you, Eli, to tell him where Tolkien had free-running horses."

Eli wished that the stars were brighter, wished that he could see Ryder Davis's face, see if truth was written there.

"And where's this supposed to have happened?"

"One time on that ridge north and west of the buildings. You were sitting on that little rock outcropping watching Runs Toward work cattle below. Stringer Jack told you not to turn around. Told you that you wouldn't be hurt, but if you wanted some extra money you could trade information for it, no questions asked. I was right behind him, watching the whole thing."

Eli's voice turned scratchy. "I was thinking about how I was going to give Runs Toward something better than I had."

"You don't have to feel guilty about it, Eli."

"Like hell I don't."

In the darkness, Eli's sigh sounded like a breeze moving through the juniper.

"You didn't hire on to move that gray."

"No, I relieved the rider of his responsibility for that magnificent horse."

"You kill him?"

"No. What do you think I am?"

"You didn't hesitate a second to do in the 'breed."

"LaFontaine?"

"Yeah."

"He was one of my best friends."

"You had one hell of a way of showing it."

"Yeah."

Silence stretched again.

"I promised him, Eli. He lived in mortal dread of being hanged. Had something to do with the Indian side of him, walking around in the hereafter with that damn rope dragging behind him . . . Something like that. So he made me promise that if it came to a hanging I'd shoot him first."

"You were just keeping a promise?"

"Yeah."

"So you just had the gray stored at the 'breed's cabin?"

"No, I was living there."

Gilfeather chuckled. "Well, I'll be damned. You sure have the wool pulled over Old Man Tolkien's eyes."

"He ever figures it out, I'm dead."

"Me, too."

"Yes."

"So what do we do?"

"Well, Eli, I've got friends down there. But they're spooky; if I try to sneak up on them in the dark, they'll shoot me. If I try to warn them now, Tolkien will shoot me and them. So, I'll wait till daylight and try to get as many of them out of there as I can.

"You can just sit up here and shoot at magpies. Just make it sound like we're both in the battle."

"Davis?"

"Yeah."

"Why are you a rustler?"

"Wild blood, Eli. Besides, I'm having one hell of a time. One hell of a time."

CHAPTER 15

THE FOUR HORSES had fought him during the first hour, unwilling to leave their band. But they had settled now, as horses do, to work the will of the two-leggeds.

The two roans were draft animals, heavy-boned and roman-nosed, big feet slapping little puffs of dust from the prairie. The dun and gray would serve either in harness or under saddle.

They were fine animals, young and strong, with muscles rippling beneath shiny coats. Runs Toward had chosen them well. He was pleased with the animals, pleased with a morning bright with sun and clear air.

Runs Toward felt cleansed of his guilt—or not cleansed so much as at ease. There is freedom in the acceptance of death, and the young Cree felt that as he rode.

The horses represented freedom. The Wilderses would be free to leave that strange tree on the prairie, free to step beyond one stage of their life and into another.

The horses represented death for Runs Toward. If he were found driving them from the Trident, he would be hanged. But he would be hanged anyway. The dreams had told him that.

He had watched the band of horses for some time, scanning the countryside for any sign of riders. But the horses were free and alone on the prairie. He circled the band, putting the Trident at his back so that when the horses ran, they would run away from Old Man Tolkien and Eli Gilfeather and the others.

They didn't run long, their freedom as much an illusion

as his life, their escape dribbling off into little knots as they snatched at bunchgrass.

One cannot run from life—or death. Runs Toward knew that, now. He had run from his fate on the Musselshell, grasping at life while his people died. He had loved life then, and he loved it still, chewing it as he chewed the licorice Eli brought him when he was a child, knowing that its sweetness was a treasure, however brief. But he had outgrown licorice. And he was losing his taste for life.

Runs Toward filled his lungs with the sweet air and the scent of the horses. It was tinged with the bouquet of sage and juniper and excitement. The animals seemed to sense that they were on an adventure, too, sprinting ahead at times, kicking up their heels at others.

The Wilderses stood, watching the plume of dust as it neared their camp.

"Is it him, Mommy?" Rosie asked, shielding her eyes from the sun with her hand.

"No, I don't think so," Sarah Wilders answered.

Jimmy waited as the horses neared. "One rider and horses, Ma. Just like Pa promised." Jimmy's voice broke. "Do you suppose it's Pa? Do you suppose he just got held up somewhere, and now he's coming with the horses?"

The prairie sun had kissed Sarah Wilders's face, shining it like a fresh autumn apple. She glowed, hope shining through the desperation that had ridden her so long. "He's certainly in a hurry. Look at all the dust."

The children picked up the excitement in their mother's voice, and Rosie danced a little jig. "Poppy's coming home. Poppy's coming home," she sang over and over. "Poppy's coming home."

"Four horses," Jimmy said. "He's riding one and driving four others."

"Look how they run," Sarah said. "They seem as excited as we are."

"Yahoo!" Jimmy shouted, tossing his hat high in the air. "Yahoo! Runs Toward must have found him. Do you suppose he was lost?"

"Your father, lost? Don't be silly. Look how far he brought us without getting lost. All the way from Nebraska to Montana. All the way to a new life."

"Yahoo!" Jimmy shouted, and Rosie joined in, "Yahoo! Yahoo! Yahoo! Yahoo!" The children and their mother joined hands and danced in a circle.

Sarah let go of Jimmy's hand, holding on to Rosie's, and they began to run toward the approaching cloud of dust, toward the return of their husband and father and the repairing of their torn lives.

Never had their feet skipped so lightly across the earth, their thoughts buoying them so that it seemed they might fly. But after they had run for only a few hundred yards, Jimmy slowed, pulling the line of excitement back to earth, back to reality.

"It isn't Pa," Jimmy said. "It isn't."

Runs Toward watched the Wilderses dash toward him and then sag as though someone had cut their puppet strings. He slowed the horses to a walk, and as he approached the family, he could see that Rosie was crying and Jimmy and Sarah seemed to be wilting into prairie earth.

Runs Toward reined to a stop, the horses he was driving skittish and dancing in front of these strangers.

"What's wrong?"

"You didn't find him, did you?" Sarah asked, her voice as lonely as a winter wind.

"Yes."

The word spoke volumes. That single word, laced with melancholy, told Sarah Wilders that her husband, provider, and confidant was dead.

She sank to her knees and wept, sobs lost in the breadth and depth of the Montana prairie. Jimmy and Rosie realized what her grief meant, and they began to cry too. She wrapped her children in her arms and the family's anguish poured from them with a force that shook their bodies.

And without thinking, Runs Toward stepped from his horse and joined the family, encircling them in his arms, his tears joining their own. He wanted to tell the family the truth, that Samuel Wilders had been hanged by the Trident crew. He wanted to say that he was a member of that party. But Jimmy and Rosie and Sarah were staring at him, asking him to make sense of Samuel Wilders's death, and the truth stuck in his throat. Runs Toward couldn't tell them that he stood by helplessly while Wilders died a violent and senseless death.

Instead, he lied, using part of a true incident, something that happened the first time the cattle had run when he was on night guard. He changed the names and embellished the story so that it would ride well on the Wilderses' ears, so that it would soothe their grief.

As he began, he was amazed at how facilely the words came. "Well, I got this secondhand, but the boss man told me that they were gathering cattle to move to a new range. Something spooked them, could have been a rattlesnake, bear smell, any . . . darn thing.

"Well, they were running down Crazy Woman Creek. Like a big flood, boss man said. He tried to turn the herd, but they kept running, swept him right up with them. Horse was getting jostled all over, horns everywhere.

"Well, he felt the horse stumble, and he figured he was dead."

Runs Toward stopped, turning to stare at Sarah Wilders. "You know what he told me?" His voice dropped to little more than a whisper. "He told me that he didn't mind dying so much. He figured that the next place was going to be better than anything he'd had so far. It was just that he hated to go when he had so much to do. Said he had always wanted to hold a baby that was his own. Isn't that the strangest thing? Said he wanted to pay people back for some of the nice things they had done for him. This boss man, he said he had a friend, almost like a father."

Runs Toward stopped and stared at the horizon as though he expected to find the words he was seeking written there.

"No, not *like* a father. His father. Anyway, the boss man said he had never told his . . . father how much he . . . appreciated everything he had done. That boss man was thinking about all those things as that horse started to go down. And just as he was about to say hello to the Lord, someone's right arm comes out of nowhere and grabs him.

"Now, the boss man, he isn't very big, and this stranger carries him one-armed right through that herd of stampeding cattle, but just as they get to the edge, the stranger's horse stumbles and goes down.

"Well, that stranger throws the boss man one-armed, just like he weighed no more than a pillow, but there's no one to throw the stranger to safety and he goes . . . under."

Sarah Wilders's chin had come up as he told the story, and Runs Toward could see that she would have expected no less of her husband. Jimmy's jaw had set, and Runs Toward could see that he was thinking that he, too, would have run into that herd to save a cowboy's life.

"Couldn't the boss man have pulled him out?" Rosie asked, sobs racking her little body. "Couldn't he have just shoved some of those cows out of the way and saved my . . ."

Rosie's voice broke into shards and fell on the prairie grass. She pressed against her mother's hip.

"The boss man hit his head on a rock when he fell. Knocked him out."

Runs Toward tried to swallow, wished he had a long drink of cold water to wash away the knot in this throat.

"Boss man said that when he came to, there wasn't anything he could do for the stranger. Said he was lying there on the prairie, bad hurt, but . . ."

Runs Toward stopped and looked deep into Sarah Wilders's eyes. "But he looked as though he was at peace with himself. Said the stranger was smiling kind of gentle-like. Told the boss man that his name was Samuel Wilders.

"Boss man asked if there was anything he could do. All that stranger said was: 'Tell my wife and children that I love them, and that I didn't mean to leave them alone.' "

The words came easily to Runs Toward. He had heard them spoken so many times in his dreams that they rolled off his tongue like the liturgy in a familiar church service.

"Take us there," Sarah Wilders said solemnly. "We have to see where they've laid him."

"Are you sure you want to do this?"

Sarah Wilders looked at Runs Toward as though she could not fathom the question.

"How can I, how can my children, leave without seeing . . . without seeing where Samuel is . . ." the sentence drifted into nothingness.

"They did what they could to make it right."

"That's what we will do, too."

Runs Toward nodded.

To ride back to the Trident aboard a horse bearing that three-pointed brand was the same as signing his own death warrant. But he couldn't very well argue that point now.

Delivering Samuel Wilders's message had been the least he could do for the man he had helped to hang, and now Runs Toward was about to do the most he could. He would ride back to the Trident astride a stolen horse, and he would die to ease his guilt. He would die so that this woman, a fierce smile locked on her tear-streaked face, could say good-bye to her husband; he would die so Samuel Wilders's grave would not be lost forever on the vastness of the Montana prairie.

"The boss man wanted to do something for . . . Mr.

Wilders. So he gave me these four horses to use, and this money." Runs Toward pulled out his life savings and handed the worn bills to Sarah Wilders. "He said he would do more if he could, but that's all he had."

Sarah looked unbelievingly at the money, and then at Runs Toward. "He must be a wonderful man."

"He said he knew that he could never make it right, but he wanted you to have the use of the horses and the money. He said when you were done with the horses, you could just let them go wherever they were and they'd find their way back to the ranch."

"Could we stop so I can meet him and thank him?"

"Uh, no, ma'am. He's . . . uh . . . got business . . . in Chicago."

"Is there an address where I can write?"

"Uh . . . no. He's dying of consumption, and he's going home to be with his family for his last few days."

"His family? Perhaps I could write to them, and—"

"I'm sorry, ma'am. I'm kind of befuddled. I didn't mean family. I meant his lawyer. He's just trying to get everything straightened out before, well, you know."

But it was plain from Sarah Wilders's expression that she didn't know, so Runs Toward forged on.

"Ma'am, I really didn't know this man. People are always bringing their herds in here, setting up camps and hoping to make their fortunes.

"It looks to me like this was the boss man's last chance, like he was trying to make peace with himself. Most likely, when he leaves, everyone else on his place will pull out, too. It's just the way it is out here."

Sarah Wilders nodded, but Runs Toward could see that something was bothering her. His mind slipped through his impromptu speech, wondering if he had let some clue slip about what really happened to Samuel Wilders, some clue that would damn him forever in this woman's eyes.

*   *   *

Runs Toward pulled his gray to a stop. From the vantage point on the edge of the hill overlooking Crazy Woman Creek, he and the Wilderses were a little above the tallest cottonwood on the creek below.

The heat of the day drew cooler air up the wash from the creek bottom, much as a flame draws wax from a candle, and Runs Toward welcomed that. But the breeze also drew the redolence of raw earth, the creek bottom a ragged wound cut by cattle hooves. The cottonwoods stood dignified, separate from the torn earth at their feet.

Riding into the creek bottom was akin to riding into a grave. Runs Toward turned to face the Wilderses behind him. "It's steep here. Jimmy, there's nothing wrong with holding to the horse's mane when you're riding bareback."

Runs Toward nudged the horse over the edge then, the gelding bracing himself against the steepness of the hill. The horse's hooves kicked up a tiny cloud of dust, borne uphill by the breeze from the bottom.

The gelding slipped a bit when he reached the bottom, and Runs Toward spoke softly to the animal, reassuring him as he reined his mount around to watch the others come.

Rosie was smiling with the adventure, and Runs Toward thought, *She doesn't know—none of them know that we have reached the end of our journey.*

Jimmy pulled his horse to a stop, and Runs Toward nudged his gelding upstream toward Samuel Wilders's grave.

The soil at the bottom of the creek was a pattern of red and gray, red where little puddles of water collected in the tracks of passing cattle, gray on the top where the dry summer winds dried the soil into a sterile cake.

Runs Toward stopped at the foot of a little ridge that hid the wash where Wilders lay; here he turned toward the others. "He's here."

They rounded the ridge. In even the past few days, the

grave had taken on a certain solidity. Runs Toward heard the breath escape from Sarah Wilders's lungs.

The creek bottom was silent, devoid of the songs of birds that would have graced it in healthier times. Each sound—Rosie asking for help to dismount, the creak of the saddle as Sarah Wilders stepped down—seemed magnified in that silence.

The three Wilderses stepped to the grave and looked down, seeing the face of their husband and father etched in the stones at their feet.

"Did he say the words?"

"The boss man?"

"Yes."

"It wouldn't hurt to say them again."

"Would you join us, Mr. Runs Toward?"

"Yes, ma'am. That would please me."

They gathered around the tombstone, taking one another's hands so that they formed a ring over the grave.

Sarah Wilders's voice came then into the creek bottom: "Dear Lord, we have come here today to say good-bye to our beloved husband and father. Although he lies here now, he will live forever in our thoughts. We need not tell you that Samuel Wilders was a good man. It is your place, not ours, to judge that.

"His life was a testament of his love for each of us and for you. Samuel Wilders was not a farmer, but he planted goodness on this earth. That goodness has taken root in the young lives here. That goodness will live forever.

"Please, Lord, take him into your arms and bless him with your warmth and love, and tell him that there will always be a place in our hearts for him. Amen."

The "Amen" hung for a moment in the air, and then Sarah Wilders opened her eyes.

"Jimmy?"

The muscles of Jimmy's jaw were knotted, and his eyes squeezed shut. To speak would open the floodgates of the emotions that threatened to spill out of his young body. He could manage only to shake his head.

"Rosie?"

The words came thin and fragile as a strand of spider's silk, shivering in the prairie wind. "We miss you, Poppy."

A shudder racked Jimmy's body, and he sagged, only his mother's hand holding him upright.

"Could I say something?" Runs Toward asked.

Sarah nodded.

"Forgive him, Lord, for any trespasses he may have committed"—Runs Toward turned his head until he felt the rays of the sun on his face—"and please forgive those who committed trespasses against him."

When Runs Toward opened his eyes, Sarah Wilders was staring at him.

"I would like to spend the night here, Mr. Runs Toward. One last night . . . with my husband. One more night before we go back to the tree."

"And then where, ma'am?"

"I don't know, Mr. Runs Toward. I just don't know."

The hill above Samuel Wilders's grave was two-tiered. Frost and water and wind chewed their way through one slab of sandstone before reaching the next. Runs Toward had chosen to build the fire there, where the light was not likely to be seen by anyone on the prairie above.

Sarah Wilders sat across the fire from Runs Toward, light and shadow teasing the young Cree, revealing and then concealing her face.

"What is this place, Mr. Runs Toward?"

"Ma'am?"

"If someone were to say to me, 'Where is your husband buried?' what would I tell him?"

Runs Toward stirred the fire, and then threw the stick into the flames. "About nine miles upstream from the mouth of Crazy Woman Creek, on the east bank."

"Whose ranch is this?"

"Nobody's. Not really. Trident has it claimed, but I'm not sure anyone really owns land."

"Haven't you ever wanted a ranch of your own?"

"Eli and I talked about it."

"Who is Eli?"

"Eli is my father now."

"He wasn't always?"

"No."

"How is it that you have two fathers?"

He told her about that day on the Musselshell, about the wolves and the death of his parents.

Sarah Wilders's next question came whispered. "How long were you in that tepee with your family after . . . ?"

"After they passed over? I don't know. It seemed like a long time. Sometimes they talked to me, telling me that it was warm and that there was feasting in the hereafter. They told me that they missed me, and that I should come to visit them.

"Sometimes I wished that I could, but I felt so weak—too weak, maybe, to die."

Sarah Wilders whispered, "I know that feeling. When Samuel disappeared, and I was left alone with the children . . . I . . ."

"I know," he said softly. "When Eli came, I thought he was death come to collect me, but he gave me life. He became a father and mother to me."

Runs Toward stirred the fire. When he next spoke, his voice was dead, devoid of expression. "I think I was meant to die that day on the Musselshell."

"You don't know that. Perhaps God had a reason for you to live. Perhaps he saved you so you could save us."

Runs Toward stirred the fire. He said nothing more.

CHAPTER 16

ELI GILFEATHER SQUEEZED his Winchester until his knuckles turned white. "Stars have disappeared. It'll be light in a few minutes."

Ryder Davis swiveled toward Gilfeather. "You anxious for this dance to begin?"

"Hell, no. I'm just tired of waiting."

"Yeah. Well, it won't be long now."

"You ever been here before?"

"Sure."

"What will the setup be?"

"Most of them will be in the cabin at one side of the corral. Other side of the corral is a kind of rough stable. They keep a tent, too, some way from the cabin."

"How many?"

"How the hell would I know?"

"Sorry."

"Eli?"

"Yeah."

"There's something I'd like to set straight before the shooting starts, just in case . . . well, you know."

"Yeah."

"Rustling is wrong, I know that, but hanging people without a trial . . . that's wrong, too. I know some of those people down there, and most of them are pretty decent. They didn't mean to be rustlers any more than most of these poor souls meant to be vigilantes. There's some hard cases, too, on both sides—people who'd shoot you in the back for a dollar, but . . ."

"But you're going down there."

"Yeah," Davis said. "I don't want to be here, but now that I am, I'll do what I can. I'm not going to shoot any rustler or any vigilante, but I'll do what I can.

"When it starts, Tolkien will be concentrating on the cabin. Not much I can do for Stringer Jack and the others in there, but I might be able to get some out of the tent. As soon as the confusion starts, I'll slip down and keep to the bushes. You shoot high as you can without looking suspicious."

"Can I shoot Tolkien?"

"You know you won't do that."

Gilfeather sighed. "Yeah, I know."

"Eli, when the shooting starts, don't stay in one place too long. Just shoot once or twice and then move. Otherwise, one of those sharpshooters down there will spot you and put you away."

"I know."

"If I don't get out of this thing . . . well, you're all right in my book."

"You, too, Davis."

The sun touched the eastern horizon, and the sky glowed gold. Shadows rooted in junipers and rocks and trees stretched to the west. The river bottom below was still in shadow, but the prairie was bathed in soft light.

Eli's attention was pulled toward the prairie, away from the uncertainty that lay below. He spotted movement, looked away, and glanced back. A horse and rider, silhouetted black as a piece of coal on a rainy night, were moving due west, directly toward the vigilante ambush.

Eli tugged at Davis's shirt and pointed. Davis swung around to face the sun.

The rider stopped and stretched, arms high in the air as though he were surrendering to the day.

"Two of them! See, a little behind and to the left."

"Yeah. Sentries."

"Sentries?"

"Hell, yes. Do you think the rustlers don't know what's going on?"

"Then why didn't they leave?"

"Look at the size of the herd in that corral. Must be a hundred. I'll bet they were about to run with those horses, but they waited too long. No way they'd get to North Dakota or Canada trailing that herd."

"They should've left anyway. What's more important, money or a stretched neck?"

"Hell, Eli, do you think the ranchers are the only greedy bastards in Montana?"

"I guess not."

And then from a coulee that appeared nothing more than a wrinkle from the vigilantes' view, four riders appeared, their horses lunging to reach the flat.

The sentries jerked around when they saw the riders bearing down on them. One horse spooked, launching a couple of bone-jarring hops. The rider fumbled with the reins, dropping one as he sawed the horse around to run. He leaned over the horse's neck, trying to reach the length of leather whose lack kept him from running for this life.

And then he had it. His heels rapped the horse's ribs, urging the beast to run, to carry its rider to safety. But the vigilantes were almost upon him.

Davis whispered, "They should have stayed in Missouri."

"Who?"

"That's the James brothers. Two brothers and their father came up here, probably to get shut of Frank and Jesse."

"They're related to the James gang?"

"Cousins, I think. Their father's down in the cabin. He's no rustler. Don't know how they got into this."

On came the racing horsemen, tufts of dirt and grass spraying behind as each horse reached toward its limit, feeling its rider's desperation in the beat of his quirt.

One of the riders sagged, and his horse slowed a bit, no

longer feeling the bite of the quirt on its shoulders. *Boom.* The distant crack of a pistol rolled across the prairie and crashed into the watching men's ears.

The rider was leaning from his horse in slow motion as the blood pumping into his lungs made him top-heavy and light-headed. And then he dropped, bouncing behind the horse like a sack of feed fallen from a runaway wagon.

Three of the vigilantes galloped past as the James boy pushed himself into a sitting position. The fourth stopped, the pistol in his hand pointing like an accusing finger.

Even at that distance, Davis and Gilfeather could see the boy look up at his accuser. The vigilante's arm jumped, and the boy jerked and fell forward, as though he were fascinated at something he had seen in the prairie between his feet. Then *boom!* the killing shot brought him down.

The other James boy thundered across the prairie in his race to reach the cabin. Spotting the vigilantes before he reached their positions, he pulled the pistol from his holster and shouted, "The sons-of-bitches stranglers have got us surrounded."

Boom! Boom! Boom!

The James boy was firing from this running horse at the vigilantes. They scrambled for cover just as he raced up to the edge of the hill overlooking the bottom and touched his spurs to the horse's belly. The horse leaped off the edge of the hill as though he were Pegasus taking flight to bear his rider to safety. The two seemed to hang in the air.

Boom!

A patch of red appeared on the rider's back. His arms flew out with the force of the blow, and the horse fell away from him, leaving him hanging for a fraction of a second, arms spread wide, head cocked over one shoulder. Christ crucified on a cross of air. Then he hit the bottom in a lifeless heap.

The door to the cabin opened and Stringer Jack's band

spilled out in front, most of them barefoot and clad in long johns, all of them carrying rifles.

Boom! Boom! Boom! Boom!

The shots came too fast to count, and the rustlers staggered back toward the cabin.

Boom! Boom! Boom! Boom! And then Tolkien's voice was rising above the din, rising even above the crack of the rifles. "Hold it. Stop firing."

"We're into it now, Eli," Davis whispered. "We sure as hell are into it, now. I—"

But Davis's words were cut off as the door to the cabin opened. A man, hands in the air, stepped out. He shaded his eyes with his hands, seeking life in the shadows around the cabin.

"Who's out there? Where's my boys?"

Ryder whispered, "Papa James."

"What have you done with my sons?"

The elderly man's voice seemed weak, scratchy in the morning light. And then Silas Tolkien's voice rumbled into the river bottom. "Dead."

"You killed my boys?"

"We killed two rustlers. If they were your boys, that's the way of it."

"You sons of bitches. You murdering sons of bitches."

James squeezed his forehead, as though he meant to squeeze the pain from it. He looked up the hill, shading his eyes from the early-morning light. His eyes swept the hillside and then lingered on a patch of shadow and color.

Papa James's back straightened, and he marched up the hill toward the vigilantes. He walked so stiffly, his back so straight, he seemed to be marching in a parade. And in the light of the dignity that shone from the old man, his woolen long johns took on the aspect of a uniform. He marched without stopping to his son's body, and fell to his knees.

Eli started to rise; Davis grabbed his arm.

"Where you going?"

"That old man needs some help."

"You go down there, you're dead. Let him handle this himself."

Eli settled back, eyes on the elderly man on the hill.

James lifted his head and slipped his arms beneath his son's shoulders and knees. He straightened then, staggering for a moment from the weight. The old man walked leaning backward to balance the weight of his son's body; the young man's head rolled back and forth with each step.

Tolkien's voice caught James as he stopped to push open the door to the cabin with his knee.

"James!"

Papa James, neck and shoulder muscles taut as a hangman's rope, turned.

Old Man Tolkien rendered his verdict. "You can go your own way. Just let those horses out of the corral, and you can walk away."

"You killed my boys. How in the hell can I walk away from that?"

"Any way you want. After you've dropped the gate to that corral."

James stepped into the darkness of the cabin, carrying his son. A moment later, he appeared at the front door again.

Front sights framed in buckhorns centered square on Papa James's back as he walked around the side of the cabin to the corral. He slipped corral poles from their slots and dropped the gate. The clattering of poles set dancing a hundred horses, skittish from the sound of gunshots and the smell of blood.

James circled the inside of the corral, driving horses toward the gate. The animals trotted through, stopping a short distance away to nibble at the green river-bottom grass.

James marched barefoot to the front of the cabin. He

turned at the door, shading his eyes from the morning sun as he stared up the hill.

"I'll see you stranglers in hell."

Boom!

The bullet caught Papa James in the center of his chest, and he dropped to the porch, legs twitching as life leaked from him, a spreading pool of red across weathered gray boards.

Boom! Boom! Boom! Boom!

The stranglers poured withering fire into the cabin, wood chips flying as slugs sought to break through the walls, seeking soft, warm flesh.

"Shoot high," Davis said as he slipped out of the juniper and made his way down the hill toward the tent. Already, the cloth walls of the crude shelter were torn by a fusillade of bullets, already the air was filled with the screams of dying men, but Ryder Davis was determined to help.

Eli Gilfeather picked a limb on a cottonwood tree above and beyond the tent. He squeezed the trigger and bark flew. How many shots would it take to sever the limb from the tree? He jacked another shell into the chamber and fired again. A miss. Another shell, and bark flew.

That old limb was stubborn, shredded yellow against the gray and black bark, but hanging on still. Eli liked stubbornness in a limb. Eli liked stubbornness in anything.

Gilfeather remembered Davis's warning and slithered through the wide-spreading juniper to another vantage point. The limb was hidden from his view, but if he leaned out of the shade of the juniper just a little . . . no, just a little more . . . There, he could see his target now.

Eli poked his rifle out of the shadow.

Boom!

Ryder Davis found a deer trail through the copse of willow that followed moist ground across the river bottom. He crawled slowly, taking care not to brush against the willow.

Little moved on the creek bottom, now, and anything that did triggered a barrage of gunfire from the hillside.

Davis paused at the edge of the willow thicket. A small open space separated him from a stand of wild ryegrass. Wild rye flourished in the blood-rich soil of ancient buffalo jumps. It could be that he was lying now over the buried bones of ancient buffalo. Certainly, the river bottom seemed nothing so much as a charnel house.

Davis scanned the bluffs, imagining that he could hear the rumble of primeval hooves, hear the bawls as the terrified animals were driven over the edge to their deaths below.

Yes, this could be a buffalo jump, ryegrass still tasting nutrients left by long-dead animals. Well, the soil had been replenished with blood today. Ryegrass would flourish next year.

The rustlers in the tent were shot all to hell, but they had crawled away into the brush. Davis had found two of them, setting them on a makeshift raft and pushing them into the river. The river might carry them to safety. At least they had a chance.

Chances. That was what this was about. Davis lay in the willows, weighing the odds that he could reach the ryegrass before the vigilantes on the hill spotted him. He had to try.

That open space lay between him and the little wash that would hide him as he crept back up to the juniper bush where Eli was waiting.

The shooting from the cabin was only sporadic now, and the vigilantes were seeking targets of opportunity from their positions above. Davis would never make the ryegrass, not now, and even if he did, any motion going through the grass would bring a hail of bullets from above.

Davis dropped his ear to the ground. With his eyes below the foliage of the willows, he could see the cabin, see the occasional puffs of white smoke as someone or other fired a rifle. Then he saw two men creeping up on the cabin as carefully as he was trying to creep back to the juniper.

One of the men was carrying a can of kerosene. Tolkien had decided to burn the survivors.

From their vantage point on the bluffs, the vigilantes could see the two arsonists crawling up to the cabin. Their attention would be focused on those two men.

Davis was willing to bet his life on that. He lay on his belly and wormed his way into the open area, hoping that the movement would not be discernible from above. His safety lay in moving slowly, but there was danger in that, too. The longer he lay exposed, the more likely he would be spotted.

Jick-Jack sat on the hillside, watching the drama play out below. He wished he were one of the men carrying kerosene and death toward the cabin, sneaking in below the gun ports to set the cabin on fire. Everyone's attention was focused on them.

More than anything in his life, Jick-Jack wanted attention. But Mr. Tolkien said he needed Jick-Jack with him. Old Man Tolkien *needed* Jick-Jack. That was attention, too.

The two men were almost to the cabin now. It was close to noon; the men had been awake long before daylight and there had been no time to eat and little time to sleep. Jick-Jack rubbed his eyes and looked toward the river.

There! Sunlight glinted off metal just at the edge of a stand of willows, someone was moving—

Whoosh! The kerosene flared against the cabin, jerking Jick-Jack's attention away from the willows. The cabin was old and tinder-dry. The flames crept along the ancient wood, tasting it as a diner might taste a salad before indulging in the main course.

Not long now, Jick-Jack thought. But what about that movement? He stared at the willows, just where they broke away in a little opening, just before wild ryegrass took over the river bottom. Just his imagination, that's all.

Ryder Davis squirmed up the little wash to the juniper bush. He had made it to safety.

"Eli?"

Silence.

"Eli?"

Davis studied the juniper. Had he come to the wrong bush? No, he could see the marks where he had dragged himself over the lip of the wash earlier that morning. This was the bush, but where had Eli gotten to?

Davis crawled into the bush. Eli was there, sitting up but hunched over, his face turned to one side.

Davis reached over and touched Eli's arm. Eli fell, and Ryder could see the darkening patch of blood on his chest.

He picked up Gilfeather's hat and brushed the dust from it before returning it to the cowboy's head. A cowboy shouldn't be without his hat, not at a time like this. And then the words came in a whisper: "Ah, hell, Eli. Why did you have to go and get yourself killed?"

CHAPTER 17

"AND I'M TELLING you that we don't have time."

Ryder Davis, shovel in hand, stood on a knoll overlooking the Missouri. At his feet lay the blanket-shrouded body of Eli Gilfeather.

"I have the time," Davis said. He leaned his weight against the shovel. Grass roots, tied in centuries of knots, resisted. Always it had been so, soil feeding the grass, and grass protecting the soil from harsh winds and rains and shovels.

"Mr. Gilfeather is dead, Mr. Davis. He doesn't give a damn if he's buried or not."

"I do," Davis said, the roots ripping as he tugged a shovelful of earth from the prairie.

Tolkien growled, "We have a hundred head of horses to move back to the Trident. We don't have time to wait for you to dig a grave."

Again, Davis wiggled the shovel through the tough grass to the soft soil beneath.

"You're not worried about the horses."

Davis wrestled the clump of grass, bottom up, onto the knoll and positioned the shovel for another bite.

Tolkien stepped into the silence. "Since you know my mind better than I, perhaps you can tell me what I am worried about."

Davis swiveled around to point the shovel toward the river bottom. "You're worried about the smoke from that cabin. Bodies make an awfully black smoke, don't they, Mr. Tolkien? I suspect people can see that smoke for ten,

183

maybe twenty miles. They might come in anytime and find you in blood up to your elbows."

Tolkien stretched his hands in front of him, palms out, as though he were fending off a blow. "I've no blood on my hands, Mr. Davis. I'm merely enforcing the law."

Davis cut another square through the grass thatch, grunting a little as he pulled it free of the prairie. "Nobody appointed you judge, Mr. Tolkien. You appointed yourself. And the 'laws' you enforce aren't written in any territorial code books."

Tolkien glowed red, "The laws are written in a higher book. 'Thou shalt not steal.' That should be plain enough for you."

"Seems to me there's another *law* in that book: 'Thou shalt not kill.' Better to be a murderer than a thief in your court, Mr. Tolkien?" Davis tipped back his hat to stare at the old man. "Judges should be seekers of justice, but you sure as hell don't want justice. There isn't a man jack standing here who wouldn't be swinging from the gallows if justice were done.

"You know what's burning down there, Mr. Tolkien? Your soul."

Tolkien's voice came low and ugly. "We have killed only known rustlers, Mr. Davis. No one else."

Davis spat on the prairie and wiped his mouth with the back of his hand. "What about that kid, that Simon Hardin? Was he a rustler?"

Jick-Jack Snyder spurred his horse to the front of the vigilantes and reined to a stop in front of Davis.

Davis looked up at the cowboy-turned-killer. His words came in a whisper. "Jick-Jack, you don't want to get into this. I am armed, and I am not wounded. You're not a gunfighter. You're Mr. Tolkien's executioner. Stick to what you know best."

Jick-Jack blanched, and his hand moved toward the butt of his Colt.

"No!" Tolkien stopped Jick-Jack, then stared at Davis and said, "You bury that . . . that misbegotten creature, if you must. But if anyone rides up while we're here, I will deal with him as I must to uphold the code of anonymity that we all swore in this undertaking. I take my oaths seriously, Mr. Davis."

"If someone comes, the responsibility will hang on your soul, not mine."

Runs Toward and the Wilderses stood in the shade of the great cottonwood, watching the dust plume in the distance.

"Cattle, Mr. Runs Toward?"

"Horses, I think. They're moving too fast for cattle."

"Why would anyone be moving a herd of that size at this time of year?"

"I don't know. Maybe the range wore down. Maybe a waterhole dried up. I don't know."

The plume of dust came closer, sending a wake through the envelope of lazy air that lay over the prairie, a wake too gentle to stir the silver leaves of sage but enough to set prairie flowers nodding.

The horizon played hide-and-seek with the afternoon sun, drifting in and out of view, drifting. But the plume of dust came on with a terrible resolution, as though it were beyond natural law.

"Mr. Runs Toward?" Sarah Wilders's words came soft and gentle as the day.

"Yes."

"Why did you stop?"

"Ma'am?"

"Why did you stop at the tree—that first day?"

Runs Toward tried to frame his answer as carefully as he could, but his mind seemed disconnected, drifting along the prairie with the racing horses.

"I didn't . . . seem to have any choice."

"Yes, I know. When Jolly broke his leg, I knew we had to

go to the tree. I didn't know why. Do you suppose those men will feel compelled to stop, too?"

Runs Toward shrugged, his attention focused on the dust. The young Cree felt a tightness in his chest. More than anything in the world, he wanted to climb aboard his horse and run.

He could feel the abundant life in the surrounding prairie, feel the roots of the grasses reaching for moisture in the soil. Life poured from the Wilderses, ragged still, but strong with a sense of hope.

In the approaching plume of dust, he could feel only death.

Runs Toward knew that the grim-faced men of his dreams rode with those horses. On they came; Runs Toward waited. *There*—the scratch of hemp against the rough bark of the cottonwood. Runs Toward looked up and saw, in the shadow of that great tree, a hangman's rope sailing over a branch. He blinked, and the rope disappeared.

But that plume of dust was real, and bearing down on him.

Runs Toward wanted to run, but he couldn't leave the Wilderses with the four Trident horses. He couldn't leave them to discover that Samuel Wilders was not a hero, but the victim of vigilante justice.

"Jimmy, better fill all the containers with water," he said to the boy. "We won't be able to hold the horses out when they come, and the water won't be fit to drink afterward."

He turned then to look at Sarah Wilders. "Do you have everything, everything you want to take from this place?"

Sarah Wilders nodded.

The stranglers' horses had been too long corraled. They wanted to run, and run they did. Tolkien and the vigilantes raced alongside them, keeping them lined out, making sure no horses splintered off to freedom.

The horses galloped across the prairie, the sound of their hooves rumbling like the threat of a summer storm. They raced onward, feeling their oats, glorying in the strength of their muscles, in their speed.

The riders came like a hot wind from Hades. They raced, free from the constraints of life, of gravity. Gradually the lead horses slowed to a trot and then to a walk, freedom an illusion.

Tolkien saw the tree first. He blinked, looked away, and then looked back. A tree, a giant cottonwood, on the prairie where no cottonwood ought to grow.

Runs Toward and the Wilderses were hidden in the tree's shadow, but the wagon and the horses cast shadows of their own.

"Must be water." Tolkien muttered, and then, as though to confirm his suspicions, the lead horses sniffed the air and turned toward the tree.

"Water, all right," Tolkien said to himself. His eyes swept the prairie. Compared to the rest of the range, the grass here was strong and tall. How was it that there was grass and water and no cattle? Well, he would fix that. Should be able to run five, maybe six hundred head here for a month or so if the water was good enough. Couldn't waste any time. Have to get stock on this range before someone else found the water.

But first he would find out who the hell thought they had a right to be here—on his range.

He motioned for Jick-Jack and five others to follow him. Ryder Davis followed the horseman across the prairie toward the tree.

Good, Tolkien thought. Now, he would find out what Davis was made of.

The vigilantes reined up just outside the ring of shadow cast by the tree. They sat silent in a semicircle, blinded in the bright summer light.

Runs Toward stepped beyond the shadow to face his accusers.

Tolkien nodded toward the team, already hitched to the wagon. "Trident horses. I knew it would come to this, Injun. Bad blood always shows. Well, you danced your jig. Now you and your friends can pay the fiddler."

At that moment, Sarah, Jimmy, and Rosie stepped into the light.

"Is this the boss man?" Rosie asked.

Runs Toward took another step forward, putting his body between the vigilantes and the Wilderses. "Uh . . . Mr. Tolkien, I'd like you to meet Sarah and Jimmy and Rosie Wilders. You remember Samuel Wilders from Crazy Woman Creek?"

Tolkien blinked. "Crazy Woman Creek?"

The image came back to him. A man, an obvious rustler, pleading for his life, swearing that the horse he rode was branded with a Nebraska pitchfork and not a Montana trident. And the man's dying plea.

Tolkien shook his head as though to free himself of that image. He stared wide-eyed at this woman and her children.

Runs Toward raised his voice. "I told them how Samuel Wilders lost his life pulling you out of the stampede on Crazy Woman Creek."

Tolkien stared at Runs Toward.

Rosie shrieked. "You're the boss man my poppy saved."

Tolkien's forehead wrinkled. He whispered, "Your poppy. He was your poppy?"

Sarah Wilders stepped forward. "Mr. Tolkien, I must thank you for your generosity and for the use of these horses."

Ryder Davis stepped down from his horse. "Mr. Tolkien's generosity is legend here, ma'am. He was just saying that he would like to do something for the family of the man . . . who saved his life."

Davis glared at Tolkien. "What was it you said, Mr. Tolkien? That some people think life is cheap. You said only a callous . . . person would believe that. You know, Mr. Tolkien, you just shined when you said that you didn't realize how precious life was until that stampede almost took yours.

"Ma'am, Mr. Tolkien said that if we were ever lucky enough to find you, he'd like to give you a bank draft for ten thousand dollars so you could have a new start in life."

Sarah Wilders's eyes widened. "Well, I couldn't. We could never . . ."

Davis smiled at Sarah. "Of course you can. Certainly you wouldn't deny an old man his pleasure."

And then Davis turned to Runs Toward. "We've not met, Mr. Runs Toward, but I knew Eli Gilfeather and he spoke very highly of you. I'm sorry to tell you, but Eli . . . He, uh . . . drowned while we were taking the horses across the Missouri. We rode both banks, but he was gone."

The blood drained from Runs Toward's face. "He couldn't swim," the young man said. "I told him he should learn how to swim, but he said he was more likely to get hit by lightning than drown out here on the prairie."

The young Cree's eyes glittered with unspent tears. "He was a good man. There are few enough good fathers in this world, and I had two."

Davis smiled, "He told me about that ranch you two were talking about. Said if anything happened to him, you should think about starting it yourself."

"Maybe someday." The words came choking from Runs Toward. He knew that he would not live out this day.

"Maybe now," Davis said. "Mr. Tolkien wanted to be sure that you got Eli's savings. That was five thousand dollars, wasn't it?"

Tolkien's jaw tightened. "You—"

Davis swept Rosie up on his arm and stepped over to Tolkien's horse. He set the girl on his shoulder so she was almost at eye level with the old man. "She's my witness, Mr. Tolkien. You know all about witnesses, don't you?"

Tolkien wilted under Rosie's smile. He reached out, arms shaking, and took the little girl, holding her awkwardly as his horse shied at the new weight.

The words came in a whisper, almost too soft to hear. "I'm sorry about your father, Rosie. Really sorry. I wish there was more that I could do."

When Tolkien looked down at Runs Toward, his face seemed to have been broken into shards, as though he were looking at his own image in a broken mirror.

"I intend to set things straight with you, too, Injun."

Runs Toward nodded. "I will come with you. We can settle our . . . business elsewhere." The young Cree seemed to be shining, above worldly concerns.

Tolkien's face knotted, and he shook his head. "I didn't . . . mean that."

Davis stepped into the silence. "Mr. Tolkien's right. Might as well settle up now. Climb down, Mr. Tolkien. You can write the drafts on a Fort Benton bank. While you're at it, you could give them a bill of sale for those horses."

Tolkien turned to stare at Rosie. She smiled back, "pretty as a picture."

"Yes," Tolkien said. "Yes, I can do that. That's the least I can do."

EPILOGUE

THE KILLER WINDS came in the winter of 1886–87. They howled like banshees over an earth wrapped in an envelope of cold that reached sixty-three degrees below zero.

Cattle left a prairie ravaged by overgrazing to range through Great Falls bawling for food, but there was none to give, and they died in doorways. Some cattle froze standing up, mute testaments to man's greed. In all, some 360,000 head of cattle died that year, and open-range ranching died with them.

Mother Nature had wreaked her vengeance.

Granville Stuart, one of the prominent ranchers of that time, gave up the cattle business, saying that he would never again keep animals that he could not feed.

Two men who escaped the shootout between the vigilantes and Stringer Jack floated downriver to a military fort. They turned themselves in. Later, vigilantes took these men from the custody of a federal marshall and lynched them.

The deaths of Billy Downs and California Ed raised a great hue and cry against the ranchers. When the vigilantes tracked some suspected rustlers to the Little Rockies, they were turned back by a mob of angry miners.

If you have enjoyed this book and would like to receive details about other Walker Western titles, please write to:

Western Editor
Walker and Company
435 Hudson Street
New York, NY 10014